The Guardians: **Vengeance Day**

Richard Austin is the pseudonym of a popular
science fiction adventure writer.

Also by Richard Austin in Pan Books

Richard Austin

THE GUARDIANS
VENGEANCE DAY

PAN BOOKS
London, Sydney and Auckland

For Scott Haney and his team,
good troopies all.

First published 1987 by Jove Books, a division of
the Berkley Publishing Group, New York

This edition published 1991 by Pan Books Ltd,
Cavaye Place, London SW10 9PG

9 8 7 6 5 4 3 2 1

© Richard Austin 1987

ISBN 0 330 31857 8

Printed in England by Clays Ltd, St Ives plc

PROLOGUE

They called him Cowboy. He was six foot six, and a good ol' boy. He weighed 389 pounds in his Fruit of the Looms, and a whole lot of it was fat. And a whole lot wasn't.

The wind wouldn't let him wear his frayed straw cowboy hat outside the vehicle tonight, and it was getting in his dirty-blond hair and tossing up his cowlick. His little pig eyes were watering behind black hornrims two sizes too small for his moon-pie face. His vast, bulgy, pale body was stuffed every which way into cammie pants and camouflage ski vest and a white T-shirt. He looked like he ought to be wearing overalls. He had a Red Man chaw tucked in behind his smile.

He spat a nice dark juicy one.

Little Pirelli, who looked as if he weighed maybe 120 when he was real wet, jumped about eight feet in the air and almost came down in the campfire. He spurted some Italian out of his mouth, and then settled down to cussing Cowboy in English.

"Well, now, Luigi, what's eatin' at you?" Cowboy asked. Luigi wasn't Pirelli's name, and it made him nuts to be called that.

"For Christ's sake," said Corbin, squatting down by the fire with his plateful of rabbit food and his big old fancy rifle lying on the ground beside him in its glistening sealskin case. "Give it a rest, can't you?"

"You know, you're pretty cute there, boy," Cowboy said, then grinned. His voice was kind of high for all that chest. "I always say I'm a man who'll fight or fuck most anything that moves. And I ain't never got it up no faggot Aussie traitor football star before."

Corbin turned red clear up to the roots of his hair. "You bloody bastard—"

"That's enough," said a tired voice. It was the Dutchman, Van Thyssel, the straw boss of this little outfit.

Cowboy flared his nostrils a tad, bobbed his head once or twice like a horse with a fly in its face, and said nothing.

"It's bloody freezing," Corbin said, munching on his veggie stuff like some kind of underfed squirrel. "I thought California was warm."

"It's wintertime, boy," Cowboy said.

"Where I come from," Corbin said, "it's just turning summer."

"Perhaps you would prefer to be back in Europe fighting hordes of Muslim reactionaries?" Pirelli had a funny way of speaking, not as weird as the Italian accents they use on TV, but still pretty humorous.

"Just seems damned odd to be coming ashore as everyone else is pulling out to sea," Corbin said.

"Ol' Chairman Max just bringin' in the first team, Wombat," said Cowboy, setting him straight. "You worried about comin' up to the major leagues? This ain't gonna be nothin' like lying on some old roof in Amsterdam pickin' off them housewives protesting the butter-ration cuts. These boys shoot back."

Pirelli looked at him with tiny rat eyes. "Afraid, Cowboy?"

Cowboy laughed and laughed. The surf thumped on the rocks way down at the base of the cliff, and he laughed a lot louder than that. "You know, Luigi, I ain't fucked up nobody in a coon's age. You remember that boy in Marseilles? I turned his hips around so his legs fit on backwards. Well, maybe you'd look better like that, ya think?"

He pushed off from the steel flank of the V-450. Pirelli popped up again, and started waving a little knife around.

"That there's a fine knife for cuttin' throats, Luigi," Cowboy said. "Too bad the poor thing'd just get purely lost in all my flab—"

Peter Lynch stuck his head out of the car. He'd been sitting in there picking at his corns with Luttwak, the East German. Luttwak used to spend his time teaching these nice Third World people how to torture prisoners right. Instructing them in modern police procedures, they called it, and a lot of the procedures he had learned from his daddy—who had been Gestapo, until the Russkies came pouring in and it seemed like a real good time to switch sides. Peter was the sort who looked like he ought to have an alligator patch stuck on the chest of his cammie shirt.

"Europe calling," he said in that oozy maple-syrup prep-school voice of his. "We have a target, gentlemen."

Van Thyssel looked up from where he was sitting, staring at the fire with eyes older than he was. "Mission?"

"As if our esteemed commander has to ask," Peter said. "Termination with extreme prejudice, as my colleagues in the Company used to say. Maximum closure."

Corbin put down his plate and rubbed his hands together.

The Dutchman sighed. "No atrocities this time," he said.

But Peter shook his head and smiled. "Have to make an example, old man. Chairman's order."

Van Thyssel looked glum.

But Cowboy got a big old grin as if he'd been trying to swallow a harmonica. 'Cause he loved his work.

CHAPTER
ONE ──────────────────────────

The night swirled around the cinder-block buildings of Balin's Forge in a wind that had winter in it. This
whistled and that wailed, and bits of loose wood and
iron out in the scrap yard banged against each other.
The thin-gauge metal walls of the mobile homes out
back flexed and sang like musical saws.

It was a wind that tasted, ever so slightly, of death. Of
ashes and old rot. Here in the Simi Valley, on the
fringes of L.A., a year and more hadn't been enough to
wash away the stinks the One-Day War had left behind.

Billy McKay rolled over and was awake. His first
awareness was the cool corrugation of the rubber
Pachmayr grips of his .45 in his palm. He flipped off the
safety and got around to wondering what had awakened
him.

On his cot, Sam Sloan stirred beneath his blankets
and mumbled, but that wasn't it. Nor was it the wind
prowling round about outside and singing in a hundred
dozen discordant voices. McKay had long since learned
to filter out the nightsounds.

Something was wrong.

Lying there on the ancient brass bed, he measured the distance in his mind to his big Maremont machine gun, leaning against the wall. His eyes slid across Sloan's shadowed shape to the window.

Something flitted past, breaking the bonds of starlight that joined the plain cement floor to the black and distant sky. "Sam," McKay said, the words pitched low in his chest, knowing they'd carry less well to unfriendly ears than a whisper. "Sam, wake up."

Sam murmured and rolled over.

The doorknob began to turn.

McKay lay with his breath frozen in his chest and the pistol pointed at the door. The bolt surrendered with a small snap. Slowly the door opened.

A hinge caught with a squeal.

The door flew inward and a burst of automatic fire broke the night in half.

With his rolling, slightly bowlegged gait, Tom Rogers had been walking inside the high wire chain-link fence, topped by a spiral of razor tape, which ran around the perimeter of Balin's Forge. He had a bulky green Army jacket on over his gray Guardians coveralls, and a green stocking cap pulled low on his head. He carried his Galil Short Assault Rifle in front of his hips in the patrol position, angled downward from right to left. He was not the sort of man to carry his weapon slung on watch.

He sidled between the fence and the boxy snout of a bulldozer that lacked both blade and treads. Ahead of him sprawled the low structure of the Forge proper. A kerosene lantern swung from the roof of the covered porch, scattering feeble yellow light in all directions. Dust swirled in the spastic glow.

Twenty meters away the fence right-angled to meet the office and living quarters. At the juncture a dark figure lay on the ground. Rogers stopped. His eyes, gray and expressionless as ball bearings, tracked right and left, squinting slightly against wind-blown grit. Nothing.

Hunched low, rifle ready, he ran across the beaten earth of the yard. Sure enough, there was a man lying there on his belly, one arm outflung. A riot shotgun was strapped across this back.

Rogers got down on one knee and turned him over. A splash of lamplight illuminated the round, stubbled face of Perry, one of Balin's people. He looked paler than the tricky light would account for. The front of his windbreaker was caked with dusty mud. His head lolled on a throat that had been gashed open by a single brutal stroke.

"McKay," Rogers said, subvocalizing for the tiny microphone strapped to his larynx. Even as he spoke he saw shadowy forms skulking around the trailers which housed Dr. Jacob Morgenstern and eight other Blueprint for Renewal personnel the Guardians had rescued from an Effsee convoy in San Diego. "Tom here. Trouble—"

From inside the building came the harsh stutter of a submachine gun.

Casey Wilson woke with someone standing over him. The only illumination in the room was a whisper of backscatter from the stars outside the open window. But he could smell the man, sweat and dirty wool, hear the rasp of his breathing over the soft respiratory rhythm of the woman lying by his side. And see the ghost gleam of the knife blade in his hand.

"All right, techno-pig," the man said under his breath, "here's how we deal with *you*."

Casey Wilson lacked Billy McKay's inhumanly acute senses, honed past razor sharpness by years of covert operations for the Marines' Force RECON and SOG-SWAC; he hadn't detected the intruder until the last fraction of a second. What he had were the reflexes of the best fighter pilot of his generation.

He jackknifed. His bare feet hit Rhoda in the small of the back and flung her on the floor. At the same instant his right fist shot out and buried itself in the knife-handler's balls.

A squealing wheeze forced its way out of the man's nostrils. But he wasn't out of it yet. The knife flashed a crescent, foam-pillow filling exploded all over Casey, and the man hurled himself on top of him even as gun-fire erupted in the next room.

"Say what?" Sam Sloan asked, rolling over so that the legs of his cot jittered on the floor. The thing almost went over. *The heck with Billy McKay for taking the good bed anyway—*

He blinked. The door to the hall was open. Sloan gaped past the big bed at the man standing there silhouetted against a vague glow from nowhere in particular. Then McKay was rolling at him like a horizontal avalanche. The huge former Marine vanished from sight, and suddenly the room was lit by a stroboscopic orange glare as the intruder chewed up the mattress with a wild burst from an Uzi.

"Jesus!" Sloan yelped. He threw himself away from the door. He crashed down hard on the cement floor, and the cot flipped over on him.

McKay lay on his belly on the icy floor. There were 9-millimeter bullets going everywhere, but none had found him yet, thank God. The roar of the submachine gun was hideously loud, unbelievable, like the devil farting right in your face. Having an automatic weapon fired at you from two meters away was enough to make an impression even on William Kosciusko McKay, the Maximum Marine and leader of the ultra-elite Guardians.

But not enough to put him off his stride. He got his Colt out in front of his face and peered beneath the bed.

The Uzi went silent. The man in the door was blowing like a Thoroughbred at the end of a furlong. "Come on out, you fascist techno-freaks," he said huskily. His voice sounded distant and tiny through the ringing in McKay's ears. "You can't hide for fucking ever."

McKay lined up the three tiny will-o'-the-wisp blobs of the self-luminous front and rear sights on his Colt and squeezed the trigger twice. A .45-caliber pile driver slammed into the gunman's right shin just below the knee. He went down screaming and thrashing. The Uzi clattered on the floor.

McKay fired twice more. The screaming stopped.

While his buddy crouched at the foot of the steps, a Winchester lever action at the ready, the black-bearded man opened the flimsy screen door of the trailer with his left hand. His right held a modified Remington 870 police shotgun by the pistol grip. The butt of the extended Choate folding stock rested in his elbow. He felt tough, invulnerable.. It was good to be back in action on the right side again. Having to help one set of would-be earth rapers against another had grated on him, as it had on all the Sons of Hayduke. And now that devil's bargain was ended.

He gingerly tested the inside door. Locked. Not surprising. He reached into his Army surplus jacket and pulled out a stiff plastic rectangle. A credit card, now obsolete. He grinned to himself; it was always a trip to turn pig-consumerist America's gimcrackery around on itself—

Two bullets struck him just under the right shoulder-blade, so close together the entrance wounds almost ran together. They were both moving better than twice the speed of sound, easily fast enough to produce a hydro-static shock wave that caused a woundchannel like an elephant gun. One of them nicked bone and tumbled. They turned his heart to pudding in passing, and he had time to feel surprise but not pain, and then he was dead.

His friend snapped the Winchester to her shoulder. An orange muzzle flash ballooned. A good shot for a snapshot reply to a muzzleflare glimpsed from the corner of the eye. But not good enough.

The round-nosed .30-30 slug whanged off the housing of a derelict generator twenty meters away. Tom Rogers let go a measured four-round burst. The rifleperson went down.

Startled cries echoed up from between the parked trailers as Tom faded into the shadowed scrap as effortlessly and completely as water into a pool.

"Jake!" The cry echoed up the corridor outside even as McKay's gunshots reverberated down it.

Sam Sloan was locked in mortal combat with his cot. He finally knocked it free with a frantic sweep of his arm and went crawling around, scrabbling for his Colt Python, which had been under the cot in its holster.

He found the piece and wrenched it out. He reared up to a kneeling position several feet behind the bed. McKay was still groveling on the floor, aiming his pistol beneath the bed at the door.

"*Jake!*" Footsteps thumped down the hall. A gangly figure appeared in the door, head a nimbus of curly hair and beard. Booted feet skidded on a carpet worn to threadbare slickness by innumerable feet. An arm windmilled an AKMS assault rifle with its stock still folded for balance.

Sloan shot the newcomer twice in the chest with the big .357 Magnum. The rifle went clattering away. The man sat down against the far wall of the hallway with his back in a smear of his own blood, feeling at himself with great curiosity.

Sloan covered him, not quite having the heart to finish him off. McKay picked himself up, tucked his .45 back under the mattress on the side away from the door, scooped the pocket-calculator-sized communicator from a bedside table made out of a cable spool. He slapped the sticky bone-conduction earphone to the mastoid process behind his left ear, then stuck the mike to his throat. The communicator itself he rolled into the left sleeve of his T-shirt as if it were a pack of cigarettes.

Hastily, Sam followed suit. Long months of training had engrained in him the truth that instant and reliable communications were the Guardians' biggest edge over their opponents. Doctrine was that their comrades could fend for themselves long enough to get in touch with them and find out what the hell was coming down.

"—trailers," Tom Rogers's voice said in his skull when he pressed his own phone into place. "Don't know how many."

"On our way." McKay's words were inaudible across the tiny room, but Sloan could hear them clearly over his communicator. McKay collected his lightweight M-60, checked the plastic half-moon-shaped ammo box hung on the side of the gleaming black receiver, then went swiftly out into the hall clad only in T-shirt and skivvies.

As he passed the second would-be assassin, who was still exploring himself and sort of gurgling, he smashed the black steel butt plate of the Maremont into his temple. The man drummed heels on the wasted carpet and toppled over. McKay drove on.

Sloan ordered his stomach back into place and followed.

Casey Wilson's head was full of the fumes of his attacker's bottled courage. The dude was lying full-length on top of him, and for all Casey's wiry strength he couldn't dislodge him. Casey had his knife wrist in his left hand and was keeping the blade from his body as best as he could. Meanwhile he and his partner were clawing for one another's eyes and Adam's apples with their free hands, and fending attacks with their elbows.

Suddenly, Casey heard a noise like an ax hitting wood. The man on top of him drove his pelvis savagely

into him, as if he were trying to rape him. Then he rolled
onto his back, clutching at his head and emitting a high
keening sound.

Rhoda was standing over him. Her red hair hung in
her face like tattered curtains. She was naked, her body
pale. Her large breasts swung as she raised Casey's
Smith & Wesson .44 Magnum by its long barrel, held in
both her hands.

The knife man had his eyes open, peering wildly between his fingers. He squealed through his nose as she
brought the huge handgun down hard and he tried to
whip his head aside. The pistol butt caught him on the
bulge of his forehead. Casey winced as he heard fingers
break.

The man convulsed and rolled off the bed. Rhoda
straddled his thrashing body. Very methodically, as if
driving a nail, she battered in his head.

Sam came through the door, which had been standing
ajar, the vented barrel of his Python twitching this way
and that like an insect's feelers. He took in Casey sitting
on the bed and the tall young woman sitting on the floor
on the other side of it.

"You okay?" Sam asked. Casey nodded. "Tom says
there's someone after the trailers."

"I'm on my way." Casey's sniper rifle stood against
the wall. He picked it up, switching on the electronic
sight.

He glanced down at Rhoda. She sat with the heavy
pistol resting on her shoulder like a baseball bat, staring
meditatively down at the man on the floor. He didn't
seem to be moving any more.

Casey ran out the door.

"Holy God, Frank," muttered the man hunkering
down beside the crude concrete pier on which one end of
the mobile home rested. "What're we going to do?"

"Keep calm," said the man behind him.

He gripped his rifle so tightly that his knuckles

threatened to burst through the skin. "That's easy for you to say. But they know we're here. There's shooting everywhere, and—"

He felt a firm, powerful hand on his shoulder. "Just get a hold of yourself, Paul. Keep your voice down. There are more of us than there are of them. And the earth's on our side."

Paul breathed heavily through his mouth, half reassured, half irritated. Frank's confident calm was contagious. But this wasn't like blowing up construction equipment or setting fire to Winnebagos parked at campgrounds. These people were *shooting back*.

"They stopped shooting, Frank," he said, extending his head on his neck to peer around the end of the foundation. He saw lots of nothing. "Maybe we should make a break for it now. Uh, Frank? Frank?"

He glanced over his shoulder. Frank's form bulked familiar, squatting down against the side of the trailer. But maybe it was more bulky than it should be. And why did the front of his shirt glisten all wet like that?

Frank slumped to the ground. But there was still a figure crouched there right behind him. With a two-edged blade in his hand.

Paul started to turn. The blade darted forward and buried itself into his kidney. His mouth flashed open to scream with the worst agony he'd ever known, white hot, worse than he could have imagined. The edge of a hand jammed itself between his jaws, muffling his scream. Then there was a second explosion of pain in his throat, and his consciousness drained out from behind his madly staring eyes.

The wind banged the open screen door of the trailer to an irregular beat. Captain Sierra stared down at the bodies of his two comrades, lying in disarray across the foot of the rickety wooden steps where a burst of machine gunfire from the main house had caught them. Then he cranked his captive's arm a few degrees higher behind her back and pushed her out on the landing.

"All right, you assholes, listen up," he shouted over the wind's many voices. "I've got one of your precious pig scientists here. You fuck with me, I'll fertilize this place with her fucking brains." For emphasis, he dug the twin muzzles of the sawed-off 12-gauge shotgun up under the hinge of her jaw until she gasped in pain.

For a moment, there was nothing but the clatter of the free-swinging door. Then somebody from the house yelled, "Just who the hell are you anyway?"

He goaded his captive down the steps. She was middle-aged and a bit overweight and stooped over from the hammerlock; she took them nice and slow.

"I'm Captain Sierra, commanding combat elements of the John Muir Brigade of the Sons of Hayduke," he shouted. He guessed that his "combat element" was pretty much dogmeat by now. Oh, well—you had to expect a few casualties in the fight for wilderness.

"What's all this about?" a second voice yelled. It had a touch of Midwestern twang to it. "Why are you doing this?"

Sierra laughed. "You didn't think we were just going to let you and your scientist pals run loose trying to turn California back into a technological wonderland, did you? Once the Effsees decided to pull out, you'd outlived your usefullness. And those scientists were just too damned dangerous to let run around loose."

"So you betrayed them to the Expeditionary Force," the second voice said.

"Yeah. Only the Effsees screwed up. If you want the job done right, do it yourself, like they say." He reached the foot of the steps and half hoisted his captive over the bodies.

"And you fucked it up all by yourselves." The first speaker stepped into the kerosene lamplight. It was a big son of a bitch in his underwear, carrying a machine gun and smoking a cigar.

"Back off, cocksucker! Me and my people are walking out of here," Sierra yelled just in case he had any people left.

The big dude shook his close-cropped head in disgust. "Give it up, asshole. You ain't got a chance."

Captain Sierra gouged with the shotgun. "I've got a hostage."

"And we," the big man said, "got a sniper."

And he let Captain Sierra register his shit-eating grin, and then a heavy-caliber bullet hit Sierra in the eye and pretty much evacuated the right hemisphere of his brain.

Ten minutes later Casey returned to his room. Rhoda still sat, stark naked despite the nocturnal chill, on the far side of the bed. She was still raising the pistol metronomically and bringing it down again with a mushy impact.

Carefully not looking at the floor, Casey came around the bed. He caught her wrist and gently pried her fingers from the Smith & Wesson's barrel. He set the pistol down on the floor.

She looked up at him. She usually had a natural vivacity that seemed to bubble out of her like a spring, but it had been in short supply since she had been raped by FSE troops four weeks before. Now her eyes were sad, and tired, and red.

She looked down at the mess on the floor. "All I could think about was when those—those men came, you know? And how powerless I felt," she said in a voice like beaten lead.

Gently, Casey stooped, and helped her to her feet. She clung to him as if she might drown.

CHAPTER
TWO

"Chairman Maximov."

Yevgeny Maximov, absolute master of the Federated States of Europe, turned away from the full-length mirror, to the twittering dismay of a flock of tailors hovering around him like hummingbirds about a portly feeder.

"Ah, Nathalie, *ma petite,*" he said, savoring the look of irritation that twitched across his aide's face when he called her his little one, "how good it is to see you. Come, tell me what you think of my new uniform?"

She frowned slightly and adjusted her massive round glasses on her nose. As always, she had accentuated the solidity of her build with the aggressive drabness of her dress, all earth-tone tweeds and shoes suitable to a geriatric patient. She had orange hair, cut short. It was Maximov's conviction that she would be rather an attractive woman if she didn't apply herself so assiduously to concealing the fact.

"You look," she said, after as much hesitation as she felt even her privileged position would let her get away with, "most . . . martial."

17

"Ah, so you think?" And he raised his arms and lumbered about in a pirouette like a dancing bear, letting her see the green and black and brown camouflage fatigues with matching forage cap for which he was being fitted from all angles. "You think that, do you?"

"Er, quite."

"I will tell you what *I* think," he said, lowering his arms to his sides as he turned back to face her. "I think that I look like Fidel Castro after he grew old and fat. Now, I am in all truth fat, and I may indeed be old, much as it wounds me to admit it. But I unconditionally decline to resemble a superannuated dictator. I am a *cutting-edge* dictator."

He tipped his hat to a different angle on his huge head and studied his reflection critically. "I might also observe that I know of no environment on Earth in which this ludicrous pattern would not stand out like a bull in the Papal tiara."

His arms exploded upward from his sides. "Shoo! Away, away, all of you! Bring me clothes fit for a civilized man, something subdued and silk. I won't go about looking as though I'd answered an advertisement in the back of an American mercenary magazine."

The tailors disappeared into the cracks between the ancient clammy stones of Castle Ehrenbreitstein, which perched on a cliff above Koblenz at the confluence of the Rhine and Neckar rivers. Maximov walked heavily to a stool, propped his broad rump on it, and lit up a Russian *makhorka* cigarette.

Nathalie Frechette's snub nose wrinkled in fastidious disapproval. "Your Excellency, I do wish you'd indulge in that habit less frequently. Europe cannot afford to have your health impaired, especially at such a crucial juncture."

"Ah, Nathalie. You only call me Excellency when you wish to lecture me." He removed the cigarette from the midst of his well-groomed beard and waved it in the air, trailing a thin blue pennon of smoke. "You must keep in mind that three-quarters of the length of this cigarette is cardboard tube. This permits very little in the way of pernicious influences to reach the mouth and lungs of the smoker. In point of fact, it permits damned little of anything to reach the smoker but a taste of soggy cardboard."

He stuck the cigarette back into his mouth and drew on it with an air of gloomy satisfaction. "So. You have news for me, yes? Iskander Bey has contracted AIDS from one of his catamites, perhaps?"

She turned red. He brandished the cigarette. "Understand, child, I only say these things to alleviate the corpse-like pallor of your cheeks. You've been living underground too long."

With an effort she controlled her embarrassed irritation. "If his Excellency is at all interested, I am able to report a breakthrough in the matter of the American bandit gang known as the Guardians."

Maximov's head had started to topple toward his capacious chest as if he were falling asleep. Now he checked it, eyeing her intently through vast and shaggy brows. "The Guardians, eh?" he said, making no attempt to mask his interest.

She nodded. "For some time they have been displaying an almost uncanny ability to anticipate the movements of the North American Expeditionary Force. They have avoided traps which should have caught them and set ambushes where they had no right to anticipate success. And there have been poorly substantiated reports—rumors, really—of impersonations of high-level personnel.

"The more susceptible among our field forces—including, I regret to say, a number of ranking officers —tended to attribute this prescience to the almost mystic degree to which the Guardians were allegedly trained. I, as you know, do not believe in miracles."

"Which is to say—"

She nodded firmly. "Our communications have

clearly been compromised. I have for some time suspected this as, indeed, I surmise your Excellency has."

He nodded with heavy-lidded eyes. Quite truthfully.
He had not, as it happened, just awakened one morning
to discover he'd accidentally become the ruler of all
Europe. He was the furthest thing from a fool.

"I was reluctant to act on this suspicion," she continued, "until I could evolve a suitable explanation for
it—otherwise, it merely begs the question of the Guardians' allegedly supernatural abilities. Now my staff
and I have come up with an answer that fits the data.
Or, rather, two answers."

Maximov nodded heavily. "Proceed."

"First, during the raid on the Heartland facility in
which your operative Trajan and the American President Lowell were assassinated, the Guardians came into
possession of an armored vehicle identical in most re-
spects to the one reported destroyed by our forces in
Texas: a V-450, known as a Super Commando, and
manufactured by Cadillac Gage. This was apparently
the vehicle prepared for our own counterterrorist team,
the Liberators, which you had specifically created to
search out and destroy the Guardians."

"And who until recently I found it most necessary—"
He's almost said *expedient,* but fortunately caught himself in time; it paid to cherish his assistant's illusions.
"—to employ in a counterinsurgency role within the
Federation itself."

"Yes, of course. In any event, our reconstruction—
and intensive computer analysis confirms its likelihood
—indicates that the vehicle's quite sophisticated on-
board data base contained the most up-to-the-minute
code and recognition sequences, not just for the Expeditionary Force, but for the FSE itself."

A wine-dark flush flowed upward from Maximov's
mottled collar. "It is fortunate, indeed," he said, in a
voice hoarser than cardboard-flavored smoke could ac-

count for, "that my very good friend Trajan failed to survive the destruction of Heartland."

"This scenario fails to account for the way in which the Guardians have apparently been able to keep abreast of our communications in spite of frequent changes in the codes. Which brings me to our second discovery —and this is no hypothesis, Mr. Chairman. Our communications and computer experts have observed and traced the phenomenon: American computer specialists, using the captured code sequences and the same communications satellites, which survived the War, that our own forces relied on, have completely infiltrated our computer network."

"Hackers," Maximov said glumly. He had a firm grounding in computer science, as a cutting-edge dictator had to, enough to be able to communicate with the top-flight experts he employed, among whom was Frechette herself. He knew that despite the popular mythology which had sprung up on the subject, most unauthorized access resulted from outsiders getting hold of access codes by bribery, treachery, or theft, and not through any mystic communion with computers. But now it was clear that the Guardians, or their allies, had the whole of the FSE computer net lying wide open to them, thanks to the codes captured with the vehicle intended for the Liberators. It was obvious how the Guardians had managed to second guess the Expeditionary Force so successfully.

And the penetration would never have been detected, but for Frechette's intuition as to what was going on, and her expertise in devising a means of tracking it down. "You've traced the source of the interference?" Maximov asked.

She nodded.

"Washington?"

"No, sir. California."

He permitted himself a smile. "How convenient."

"We have also identified a second source of penetration in Colorado, less important than the first, but still significant."

He scratched his nose with a hairy finger. "Let me guess. Would that be the place at which that army of religious zealots, by whom our departed colleague Trajan was so inexplicably fascinated, met with disaster at the hands of the Guardians?"

"It would indeed, your Excellency."

He started to hoist himself up to visit the decanter of brandy resting on a shelf among the tangle of tape measures and thread. "You've instituted countermeasures, of course?"

"Not yet, Mr. Chairman."

That stopped him. "Well? Why not then?"

She allowed herself a moment to preen. "I have evolved a plan, Mr. Chairman, to enable us to use our opponents' cleverness against them," she said, her voice husky with unwonted excitement.

Tailors fluttered back into the chamber, bringing with them one of Maximov's customary suits. He grunted with satisfaction, rose, and walked over behind a Japanese screen painted with cranes taking off from a canebrake to change.

"I suppose you intend to feed them false information," he said. "It could be difficult to arrange in the midst of a war. We don't want our own communications hopelessly tangled with disinformation."

She shifted her weight from one blocky shoe to another. "Forgive me, Mr. Chairman, but I don't think you grasp what I'm driving at. You see, what I intend is to do to them much the same thing they've been doing to us."

"Yes, my child, but we don't have convenient access to their access sequences and their codes," he puffed, pulling on his trousers.

"Oh, but we do, sir."

His head popped up behind the screen like a well-groomed jack-o'-lantern. "I beg your pardon?"

She looked like a cat who had just found a stepladder left beneath the canary's cage. "We have access to that information, sir. It would seem that there are certain elements within the American capital itself who are not entirely satisfied with the present administration."

The Chairman emerged with his pants hanging open and his collar, cuffs, and shirttail loose, spreading his arms to permit his attendants to handle the detail work. "So. *So*. After I thought the whole American enterprise had ended in disaster—that recovery of the vital resources of the Blueprint for Renewal might have to be indefinitely postponed at a time when they are most urgently needed—Nathalie, I could kiss you."

"Sir!" she exclaimed, shying back. He laughed.

"Besides," she went on, trying to assume a knowing look to hide her embarrassment, "you haven't completely given up on your plans to recover the Blueprint. You have . . . assets on the ground. My own proposal makes use of them."

"Indeed," he said, lifting his chins so that a flunky could knot a tie around his bear's neck. "Since the sledgehammer worked so poorly, I decided to return to the scalpel. And how is my poor Ivan Vissarionovich, by the way?"

"Colonel Vesensky is recuperating in England from the injuries he received from the Guardians. He has made a most astonishingly rapid recovery."

"Ah, yes. Either vegetarianism or sodomy must agree with his constitution, to make him so resilient. Not that I'm tempted to adopt either expedient myself."

"Shall I dispatch him to North America, sir?"

He cocked a brow at her. "You are my chief administrative aide, and a most invaluable one, my dear. But your authority does not extend to Colonel Vesensky. You do not *dispatch* him anywhere." She dropped her eyes. "Besides, I have plans for him elsewhere."

The tailors helped him into his suit coat. He

smoothed it down over his portmanteau. "Better, much better." He turned to his aide.

"Now, before you give me the details of this little scheme of yours, tell me—just who is the traitor in Washington?"

She hesitated. An ironic gleam in his brown eyes reminded her that need-to-know considerations hardly applied to the Chairman of the Federated States of Europe.

She told him.

He tipped his head back and laughter rang around the ancient stones of Castle Ehrenbreitstein.

CHAPTER
THREE ─────────────────

The big house, way up in the woods, rested on a graded-off part of the hill, sprawling everywhere, with massive oblong redwood roof beams thrusting out over the trombé wall and sheets of glass that seemed to quiver with the wind. There were lights on inside, the wan glow of lanterns and the occasional subliminal flicker of fluorescents powered by solar accumulators whose panels sprouted everywhere like cubist mushrooms.

A kid whose body kind of sagged around the middle was slouching along the perimeter of the terrace, where it was shored up with a fieldstone bank. He had an M-16A1 slung butt upward over one shoulder, so the flash suppressor gouged him in the ass when he walked. He was alternately tugging at it and trying to twitch the collar of his coat up farther around his scraggly beard. That wind had snow in it, and the clouds had swooped in low, fat and ready to pop.

Then a hand like a cluster of steel cables caught him under the chin and jerked his head back. His throat arched to receive the slim dagger punched in from right

25

to left behind the Adam's apple. With a twist of wiry wrist, it slashed out through the front of his neck, and the blood came like a waterfall.

You don't die at once from a knife wound. Not even when the jugular's gone. And you'd be surprised at how much noise you can make with your throat cut. Real life ain't like the movies. Real death isn't either.

Pirelli may have learned a little too much about life from the works of Marx and Marcuse and Marighela, but he hadn't learned about death from the cinema. He had better training than that, and a lifetime of first-hand experience. Lots of people's lifetimes, as a matter of fact. He held the straining jaw shut on the scream that wanted to come gurgling out, pulling the kid sentry's head so far back his neck bones creaked. The kid kept rolling his eyes back at Pirelli like a frightened horse.

He was a head taller than the former Red Brigade hit man, but Pirelli hung on while the blood soaked his sleeve and the kid shit in his pants. And then it all went out of the kid, and he fell limp. Pirelli dropped him without hesitation. It's hard to *fake* being dead when your throat's torn open.

He went belly down next to the rag-limp body, in the lee of a redwood picnic table. Nobody inside seemed to have noticed anything amiss. Muffled rock and roll radiated off the huge windows, and Pirelli's lip curled. Rock music was typical Western decadence. He was a Mantovani man himself.

"Go," he whispered, waving his arm. He wiped the knife on the sentry's coat and stuck it back into its sheath. Cowboy and Lynch came over the wall and duckwalked hastily past him. Lynch carried a boxy little Jati machine pistol half as long as the silencer screwed onto the end of it. Cowboy looked more like a Sasquatch than usual, hunched beneath the weight of two big satchels slung over his shoulder.

"Moving," Pirelli subvocalized. He unslung his own silenced Franchi submachine gun. The bone-conduction speaker taped to the mastoid behind his left ear had already confirmed the others were in place: Luttwak ready to hit the back of the house, Van Thyssel and Corbin covering from the trees with machine gun and Walther sniper's rifle.

Off to the left a satellite dish cut a weird shadow out of the sky. The heavy hardwood front door, carved with scenes from some fantasy the decadent Americans relied on to relieve the boredom of bourgeois life, opened when Lynch and the Cowboy were barely eight meters away. A young man stood there with the ends of his disorderly hair glowing like a nimbus from kerosene backlighting.

Lynch swung up the Jati. It chattered like an angry squirrel, barely audible over the mountain wind. The boy sort of gasped, doubled over, then slipped back inside the doorway.

A girl screamed.

Lynch hit the porch at a bound. He fired the Finnish MP into the house. The screaming stopped, but various other voices took up the slack.

Lynch pivoted neatly to the side. Cowboy lumbered past him like a bull missing a matador, a big Cordura bag in either hand. Inside the doorway he stopped and pitched them left and right in the huge common room, as far as his tree-trunk arms could heave them. Then he and Lynch ran like crazy back toward the lip of the terrace.

Pirelli pushed himself backwards over the edge and huddled up next to the rough stone face. A moment later his two comrades thumped down on the prickly dry grass beside him.

The night seemed to hold its breath. Then two yellow flashes lit the slanting ceiling of the main room, and the trombé wall bulged outward and came shooting out through the windows in an eruption of adobe bricks and wood and body bits and shards of darkly glittering glass.

They lay where they were until the debris quit raining down on the terrace and the slope behind them, and a little bit of their hearing came back. There was the crackling of fire and moaning voices: not even two of Cowboy's special satchel charges could kill everybody in a big open room, but they surely hadn't left anyone in any shape to give the Liberators trouble when they went in to mop up. And the people in the rest of the house were probably too stunned to move for the next vital two minutes.

Pirelli jumped up. His thin lips stretched into an unaccustomed smile.

This was the part he really liked.

Billy McKay stared glumly into the heavy earthenware mug. The liquid inside looked like plain old Lipton tea, but whatever he'd just been served by the smiling young Hispanic woman in the commissary of New Eden's Main Habitat smelled like nothing in the world so much as boiled straw. Straw that had been removed from the floor of a horse's stall, after a month or so to ripen. McKay was more of a beer fan, but right now he longed for a cup of good old-fashioned orange pekoe.

"Lieutenant McKay," Dr. Jacob Morgenstern said with a precise nod as he seated himself across the wooden table. He wore his inevitable brown and black striped aba and sandals, in spite of the fact that neither the sun through the tall south-facing clerestory windows, nor the wood and methane stoves sizzling away in the kitchen, had warmed the commissary to any appreciable extent. Then again, McKay guessed Dr. Jake didn't have much circulation trouble; and never mind his age, he was an active old fuck.

"Morning," McKay grunted. His mouth twisted as

he watched Morgenstern knock back his own horrible-smelling drink the way McKay would down a mug of Coors.

The other Guardians appeared and drifted over. Tom Rogers looked wide awake and completely pulled together, but that was the way he'd look if you woke him in the middle of the night, damn him. Sam Sloan was dressed in his damned gray sweatsuit and Asics running shoes, puffing and blowing and pink in the cheeks from his morning run. He claimed dashing up and down the broad-bottomed valley in the western slope of the Sierra Nevadas was the sort of exercise they all needed after spending all their time sitting on their duffs in an armored car. But he was the kind of nitwit who ran the marathon for fun back in his Navy days.

McKay kept hoping it would snow about six or eight feet, but in his guts he knew that would never slow Sloan down. The crazed sonofabitch would do his roadwork on snowshoes, waddling like a fat Navajo woman at K-Mart, if he had to.

To McKay's relief, Casey came in blurry and saggy-eyed. It was good to see that at least one of his buddies was human anyway.

Aside from poor Perry, neither Balin's people nor Morgenstern's scientists—both of whom had suffered considerably at the hands of the recently departed Federated States of Europe Expeditionary Force—had taken any casualties in the attack on the Forge. How many raiders got away was unclear. None of the ones left behind was in any shape to give too many lucid answers before giving up the ghost. The Guardians did gather that the Sons of Hayduke's leader, ginger-bearded Neil Mixson, had been along on the raid. His body wasn't found.

Otherwise, the brief interrogation of the several mortally injured marauders confirmed what Captain Sierra had said. When the Effsees were ordered to throw in the towel and sail home to help defend the FSE itself from invasion by Muslim fundamentalist fanatics, Mixson had decided it was time to end the devil's bargain which had bound them to the Guardians and Project Blueprint in opposition to the common enemy. They had betrayed Morgenstern and the handful of Blueprint participants he had collected during the Effsee interregnum to an FSE-armored column commanded by Colonel William "Piledriver" Ramsay, but the Guardians had ambushed Ramsay in San Diego, a few klicks from where the rest of the Expeditionary Force was embarking for Europe, and liberated the captive specialists. The Sons of Hayduke, plus a few Daughters, had then decided to take matters into their own hands.

The Haydukes having dropped the ball, the Guardians had cruised north toward New Eden. En route, they had paused for a C-130*bis* Super Hercules out of Kirtland Base in Albuquerque—liberated from the Effsees over the summer by the Guardians themselves—to touch down on a rare stretch of clear highway near the Bakersfield rubble to pick up the Blueprint specialists for their long-deferred flight to Washington.

Morgenstern had refused to accompany them. He claimed his place was in California, where he had been assembling a trade network to speed recovery before the FSE invasion and leading the resistance after it. The Guardians had mixed feelings about this. On the one hand, Morgenstern was a hell of a good man, a certified genius who in his day had seen combat both as a paratrooper and a tank brigade commander. He was capable of giving the Guardians just a touch of the sense of direction and leadership they once had gotten from the mysterious Major Crenna, who dreamed up both the Guardians and Project Blueprint and gave his life for them in Heartland. Elite as they were, self-starters though they were, they needed that. Moreover, he had been intimately associated with Crenna on assembling the Blueprint, and was an invaluable source of leads and information.

On the other hand, he was an egotistical old martinet who could be one Christ-almighty pain in the ass.

Still, on balance they were glad he'd stayed.

The three Guardians sat down, blowing steam from their mugs of slightly frothy herb tea to wait for breakfast to be ready. They exchanged polite greetings with Morgenstern. Their fearless leader glowered at them.

"Ham and eggs," he said.

"Tofu," Sam Sloan said with sadistic relish. "Mung bean sprouts. Whole-grain cereal without a speck of sugar." He took a hearty swig of his drink, as if he actually enjoyed the horrible stuff. McKay was certain he did that just to piss him off.

"Yurg," McKay said.

"Think how healthy it is," Sloan gloated. "Think of all the calories and cholesterol you're missing."

"Imagine starting the day with a breakfast of rabbit food and stuff that looks like a deader who's been in the surf for a week."

Sloan clucked and shook his head.

"I don't know, man," Casey Wilson said, warming his hands on his mug and staring unfocussedly through McKay as if the enormous ex-Marine had become transparent. "I know the food here is, like, real good for you. But I could sure use a steak and fried eggs this morning."

"See?" McKay said. "Casey may be a flake, but he's got some sense in him. Trust a fighter pilot to know that a real man needs red meat. You don't raise no jet aces on bean curds and weeds."

"But that's what we're getting for breakfast anyway," Sloan pointed out triumphantly. His tone was worn rather thin, however. The fare at the New Eden

Agricultural Research Facility was getting to him, too. But hassling his leader was a matter of principle for him.

"Any word from Vista?" Sloan asked over the rim of his mug.

McKay shook his head. "Nothing yet."

"That's unusual."

"Yeah. But you know how kid geniuses are."

"Certainly I do, since I was one. Of a more modest variety than our friends in Pineholm, of course."

McKay grunted.

"Morning, everybody," a voice said.

Sloan glanced up and recoiled. Baxter was standing there, right behind his right shoulder. The informer resembled a large, ill-nourished rodent with greasy silver hair slicked back beside his bald spot, sunken dark eyes, a big mobile nose, and cheeks furred with grizzled stubble that defied razors. Despite the fact that the Guardians insisted he shower and change clothes each and every morning, Baxter's lemon-yellow New Eden-issue coveralls had a rumpled, grimy look to them. He smelled of sweat and nameless fungus that no indus-trial-strength disinfectant could touch.

"Have a seat, Baxter," said Sloan, surreptitiously checking his running suit to see if Baxter might have brushed against it and left stains.

"Downwind," McKay added.

Sloan shot him a *be nice, asshole* look. Blithely un-concerned, Baxter sat down and began to shovel up food piled on his terra-cotta plate.

Sloan took one look at the plate and shied like a horse from a sidewinder. "Sweet Jesus. What in heaven's name is *that?*"

What it looked like to him was afterbirth piled on spoiled cottage cheese. Baxter prodded the dripping red and white mess with a fork. It jiggled.

"Tofu surprise," he said. Clots of white tumbled down his moist lower lip and down among the graying thatch of his chest. "Great stuff. Mahalaby's cooking today."

The Guardians groaned as one man. Everybody took turns with the chores here in Utopian New Eden. And while the facility's director, Dr. Georges Mahalaby, might be a genius biochemist and a mortal saint, he was possibly the worst cook in captivity.

In horrified fascination, McKay watched Baxter shovel forkfuls of the goo into his face. "How can you stomach that shit, Baxter? It looks like you're the second person today to try eating it."

Baxter chewed a moment, opening his mouth at every stroke, mulling over the question. "I tell you what, son. After you've lived off what you find in the freezer cases of supermarkets that ain't had no power for two or three weeks for a spell, you get so not much bothers you any more."

McKay swallowed his stomach, which was trying to scale his esophagus and make a break for it. He'd eaten some pretty gross things in the field. But Baxter would do anything to survive. *Anything.*

He would even betray anybody's secrets. To anyone. He had recently been drafted into the FSE Expeditionary Force's intelligence service and attached to none other than Piledriver Ramsay. When it became apparent that the Effsees' star was rapidly collapsing into a black hole he'd happily deserted, and alerted the Guardians to the Sons of Hayduke's treachery into the bargain. Before that, he had at different times served the Guardians, Morgenstern, New Eden's untrustworthy neighbor General Edwards (whom the Guardians had finally had to crush for good and all, during the Effsee collapse), and the terrorist alliance with which California's mad ex-lieutenant governor, Geoff van Damm, had tried to rule the state in the name of Chairman Maximov and World Revolution, with a fine lack of partiality.

His repulsiveness was like some kind of force field. That was how McKay figured it. You kind of wanted to edit him out of reality, and so you tended to forget he was there, and say things you shouldn't. At the same time, he was in some mysterious way too gross to kill, as if you might get some of his juice on you or something if you squashed him. And when all was said and done, he was too valuable to do away with. Baxter knew everything. And what he knew, he told.

Morgenstern returned, having gotten up while everyone's attentions were on Baxter. For a man who could upstage a rock star in full cry, the Israeli economist could be pretty surreptitious himself. He sat down and began to chew a chunk of brown bread.

The table filled up with eyes. "Uh, like, where'd you get the bread, Doctor?" Casey asked.

"Asked for it."

"Think they've got more?"

"It would seem likely."

The Guardians all stood up at once and tried not to run to the serving counter.

"We've deduced the existence of another Blueprint facility," Morgenstern told them that afternoon. He'd been online to Washington for quite a while, via a satellite-relayed link. The link had originally been opened by the junior network whizzes of Vista Systems in northern California, who were the ones mainly responsible for carrying out the penetration of the vast FSE communications.

The Vista kids still hadn't been heard from, which was odd, since they usually started feeding the latest intelligence gleaned from the FSE data network early in the morning—by nine or ten anyway, which was early for them. Sloan had started getting twitchy, but he was an old woman. McKay figured they'd been up late playing Dungeons and Dragons. They'd check in after a while.

He scrunched his bulk around in one of the chairs in the small, steeply tiered lecture hall in a wing to one side of the Main Habitat. It was one of those awful seats like they have in lecture halls everywhere, two sizes too small and with a tiny, cramped writing surface that swings down impossibly close to your gut.

"I don't quite read you, Doc," he said. "The way I got it, you helped put together the Blueprint. How come you don't know more about where the pieces of it are, if you don't mind my asking?"

The doctor's wiry brows clamped down over his eyes in irritation. "Since I'm sure you've been exposed to elementary principles of security, Lieutenant, perhaps you can understand when I tell you there was a severe limit on what I knew—or wanted to know—about the Blueprint for Renewal. Not even Major Crenna, who was far more instrumental that I in assembling the Blueprint, knew where more than a fraction of the personnel and facilities were located—as you are, I believe, well aware."

McKay scratched the close-cropped side of his head. "Yeah, you're right, Doc. Forget I said anything."

Morgenstern eyed him for a few heartbeats, then nodded. He hit keys on the pad inset in the podium in front of him. A computer-generated map of the U.S. in blue glowed into life on the three-by-four-meter LCD screen that had been masquerading as blank wall behind him.

"Your objective is a factory. We have been unable to ascertain what it might produce that's important enough to account for its inclusion in the Blueprint, but the records fragments we have clearly indicate its existence. It is located—" He touched more keys and a section of the map turned yellow. "—somewhere in this region here."

The Guardians stared at the map. "Let me get this straight, Doctor," Sloan said, his drawl running slower than usual. "This factory is located somewhere between the Rockies and Minnesota, and between Colorado and Canada?"

"That is correct. As best we can determine." He scratched beneath the fringe of hair surrounding the sunburned dome of his head. "We do have data indicating that it does not lie within an urban area."

"And nobody knows what this factory does?"

"No."

Sloan's rump slid several centimeters forward on the slick vinyl seats. "And it's getting on toward winter along up there."

"That's true, Commander."

Sloan sighed. "Maybe our motto should be: 'The impossible we accomplish immediately. The ridiculous may take us a spell.' "

Morgenstern eyed them bleakly for a few moments. "I sympathize with you, gentlemen. But Washington is quite insistent that this facility be located as soon as possible. And, in fairness, it is the strongest lead we have at the moment."

It was clear from his tone that fairness to Washington wasn't his favorite posture. He claimed that the reason he'd insisted on staying behind in California was that his work was here. But the Guardians—or McKay, at least—had a sneaking suspicion he stayed because he couldn't hack Maggie Connoly. The ex-Harvard economist had set herself up as President Jeff MacGregor's chief adviser, and was now damned near running the country in a lot of ways—as much as anyone in Washington ran the country, which still was not a whole hell of a lot.

"Well," McKay said, exhaling heavily, "I guess the time has come to saddle up and go again. Ain't got nothing holding us here."

Nothing except his friend Anna Yoshimitsu, recently rescued from enforced duty as consort to Randy Bonner, one of the late and unlamented overlords of Edwards Valley. Or Susan Spinelli, the long-legged, blond assistant director of New Eden, who'd been keeping Sam company. It wasn't a good idea to get too attached to all those homey little comforts in this line of work.

"At least, we won't have Maximov's people breathing down our necks," Casey observed.

"Amen," Sloan said fervently. "Those days are gone forever."

"Maybe," McKay said, "and maybe not."

Sloan laughed. "A million Muslim fanatics are pouring into Europe, and you think Chairman Maximov is going to bother with *us?* Really, McKay, get real."

"Dream on, jerk," McKay grumbled half beneath his breath.

Scowling, he tried to stand. The desk top refused to budge, pinning him in his seat. He tried to turn it back to the vertical. It still refused to budge.

"Damn," he said and pulled. The desk top came off in his hand.

He stood up and gestured with the unmoored writing desk, which was shaped sort of like a map of Oklahoma if the state was having water-retention problems in the Panhandle.

"Hell of a way to make a living," he said.

CHAPTER
FOUR ─────────────────────

"Well, Case," McKay said, "I guess you must be itching to get back to the Freehold."

"Why's that, Billy?" Casey's voice crackled back over the intercom.

"Well, hey, how soon they forget. Does the name Angie Connoly ring any bells? Long, tall, with black hair hanging down to her ass and legs clear down to the ground."

Even though Casey was up in the turret and he was holding down the ESO's seat, McKay could *feel* the former fighter jock blush. Casey was in more than tight with the lovely young Freehold woman.

"Uh, no, Billy, I remember. Uh, that is—"

"What are you giving him a hard time about, McKay?" Sloan asked with a sneer. "I seem to remember a diminutive Chicana doctor with hair like fire and a temper to match being seen more than once in your company when we were last in the Freehold."

McKay gave him an ugly look. As a matter of fact, he and Ruby Vasquez weren't exactly strangers either. But Casey and Angie seemed fairly serious about each other.

39

Whereas McKay and Vasquez were deeply in lust. McKay preferred quiet, submissive women, ones who knew their place. He didn't see himself getting wound up with a woman who rode him like a bronc in bed and fought with him like a badger out of it.

Hell, I wouldn't put it past the bitch to wear spurs to bed, he thought. *Hasn't yet, but there's always a first time—*

He wasn't willing to cede the upper hand to Sloan just yet. "And what was my man Casey doing with Ms. Rhoda at the Forge just three nights ago? Teaching her to meditate?"

Casey started to sputter again, totally flustered. He had an open relationship with both women, with their knowledge, but McKay loved to make him defensive about it. For a fighter pilot, Casey was sure easy to rattle.

"And I suppose Ms. Yoshimitsu spent all last night in your room at the Habitat filling you in on the ins and outs of organic gardening, McKay?" Sloan asked with poisonous sweetness.

McKay folded his arms across his chest and sunk his massive chin to his breastbone. "Aw, fuck everybody who can't take a joke," he muttered.

Snow had already started to settle in on the passes through the Sierra Nevadas. That meant a broad detour to start the Guardians' latest mission. A lot of the passes closed down tight with the first snow and stayed that way till April.

The husky Cadillac Gage could bull its way through places no mere automobile could dream of going, but not even Casey Wilson felt like pressing the Guardians' luck. There were no snowplows working the passes this second winter after the War, and little hope of finding help if they got into trouble. The Guardians had no urgent desire to get their journey underway by permanently ditching their wheels in some ravine.

"Scenic Bakersfield again," McKay said. "Oh, my."

"Would you rather take your chances up north?" Sloan asked from behind the wheel. "Soda Springs is supposed to stay clear."

"Yeah. And I believe in campaign promises and the Tooth Fairy, too." McKay slouched down behind the console of the electronic systems operator's seat next to Sloan and squinted malevolently through the laminated glass-and-plastic armor block of the vision slit. Outside a half-assed early afternoon snow was drifting down into the broad tawny bowl of the San Joaquin Valley.

"Tehachapi's lots lower than the passes farther north," Casey said earnestly from the turret. "And this far south it doesn't get anywhere near the snow. In fact, it's, like, pretty unusual to be getting snow around here, but the War messed the weather patterns up and all."

"Yeah, yeah, we know that," McKay said. "But shit . . . Bakersfield. I don't blame the Russians for nuking it, even though it ain't got no strategic importance."

"Well," said Sloan, for whom the subject was wearing rather thin. "At least we can bypass the damned city."

"Yeah," McKay said. "Count our blessings, huh?"

The drill of picking their way around the masses of stalled cars that clogged the arteries surrounding all major American cities had been reduced to routine. Buzzing along the shoulder or cutting off onto lesser known and subsequently less congested county roads whose locations they got off the amazingly detailed maps hard-wired into Mobile One's on-board computer took hardly more time than if the main roads had been clear.

There were even places where a start had been made at clearing the dead cars off the highway, or grading out overland detours around the bad spots. The survivors were trying to put their lives back in order the way survivors always have and always will. In spite of the big advance billing it got, thermonuclear war wasn't that much different from the calamities that had beset mankind since it came down out of the trees. Life went on.

Eventually the Guardians worked their way around Bakersfield and onto State Road 58. They saw hardly anybody, and the few people they did see made themselves scarce—one old guy they found pumping his way toward them on the outskirts of Edison hopped right off his bicycle and went racing off across a recently plowed field like an Olympic sprinter. In their usual insightful way the Effsees had tried to use gangs of conscripted labor to clear off the roads like the old French *corvée* system. The effect of that was that the labor gangs shirked, and all the people who would normally have been working on the roads with a will hid. So the roads had been getting cleared a lot slower than they would have had the FSE left well enough alone.

News of the Effsee withdrawal may or may not have reached this far, but it was obvious that nobody was taking any chances with stray armored cars.

"Do you, like, ever wonder just why this car happened to be waiting for us in that garage in Heartland?" Casey asked the world in general, watching out the portside vision block as the cyclist crossed the field with astonishing pronghorn bounds. It was his turn to drive again.

Sitting on a seat that folded down from the hull aft of the turret roof, McKay sighed. It was a question one or another of them had been asking every week or two since they busted out of Heartland in July. Nobody'd come up with an answer yet.

"I've quit worrying about it," Sam said.

"I haven't," said McKay.

Tehachapi Pass was nice and clear as predicted. There wasn't even the dispirited drizzle of snow that had been falling in the lowlands. They were rumbling down through pine woods toward Mojave when darkness came down.

They pulled off out of sight onto a logging road run-

ning down out of the Tehachapi range. The road was
clear of underbrush, but that was probably due to the
fact that it served as the channel of a fast-flowing
stream during the heavy rainstorms that followed the
One-Day War. The wheel ruts had eroded to deep
gullies with a big hump running between them, and even
Mobile One with its high ground-clearance scraped dirt.

Casey popped out to set out a number of electronic
sensors slaved to the on-board computer, and set up a
perimeter of four claymores in a swastika pattern,
which could be touched off singly or all at once from inside the car by means of a clacker—an electronic hand
detonator.

McKay had a combat soldier's distrust for Star Wars
weaponry, so he didn't have much faith in the fancy
sensors; even with the computer's help, they had a terrible time telling a white-tailed deer from a human intruder. On the other hand, he believed in the claymores
with a devout and simple faith. Many times they had
saved his ass in the field, and they'd shortstopped a
mass rush on the Guardians during their first trip to
California a year ago.

He and Tom Rogers broke out freeze-dried rations
packs and started fixing dinner as Sam Sloan got on the
horn to Washington for the evening check-in. A maser
tight-beam caster aimed itself at a computer-chosen
point in the starry sky, and up in orbit above the
Rockies a relay clicked in a satellite. In a matter of
seconds, Washington was on the line.

"Ain't science wonderful," McKay muttered under
his breath, sliding plastic trays into the hull-mounted
microwave. "We can get nagged long distance by Maggie Connoly."

But they didn't get Maggie Connoly, just an operator
from Tide Camp, the weird military commune along the
Tidal Basin that had kept the abandoned White House
as a shrine during the year-long absence of president
and presidency. The Guardians had nothing to report.

They were still headed for the Freehold in Colorado's San Luis Valley, which they were planning to use as a staging area for their search for the mysterious Blueprint-connected factory. Their ETA was two days from right about now.

In a way, McKay was almost disappointed Dr. Connoly wasn't on the line. Because the closest thing to a head that the happy high-tech anarchists of the Freehold acknowledged was one Angelina Connoly, the doctor's very own daughter. Laissez-faire daughter and Keynesian mother didn't get along any too well, and it was always good to rub Maggie's nose in the fact. Connoly senior might be a big Blueprint wheel, but Billy McKay held her in the same wary regard as he did timber rattlers and Arab terrorists.

"Uh, Guardians, we have a message for you to contact Dr. Morgenstern at New Eden soonest, over," the Tide Camp signalman concluded.

"Say again, Washington, over?" Sloan said. The man repeated the message.

McKay was standing over Sloan's shoulder with a cigar in his mouth, just dying for this conversation to be over so he could go outside and light it. "What the fuck, over? Why didn't he call us direct?"

"New Eden says the mountains block transmission and they can't pinpoint you for a satel-link relay, over," Washington came back when the question was relayed.

"Why didn't Vista feed him our position?"

"Vista is off-line. Negative response. Better talk to New Eden, Guardians. Washington out."

Sam turned a worried look up at McKay's scowl and punched the sequence that would bounce their signal off a satellite and back down to New Eden, in the mountains east of Fresno. Susan Spinelli answered, and her voice was unsteady as a San Francisco sidewalk when the San Andreas hiccuped.

"Something terrible has happened," she said. "I—let me get Dr. Morgenstern."

The Israeli must have been awaiting their call, because even with time slowed to a tension crawl, it didn't seem long before they heard his familiar acerbic rasp.

McKay had his communicator patched directly through this time. "What the hell's going on, Doctor?"

"When we had heard nothing from Vista Systems by the time you left this morning, we sent a team up to Pineholm to investigate."

For some reason, McKay felt like gerbils were running a treadmill in his belly. "And what did they find out, Doc?"

"They'd all been killed," Morgenstern said. "To a man, to a woman. *All* of them.

Sitting at the ESO console of the V-450, Peter Lynch grinned. In the blacked-out car, the lights from the board gave his chiseled handsome features a diabolic cast.

"It's confirmed, if we needed it," he said. "They're headed for that place in Colorado."

"Ain't that the one where that crusade old Trajan put together busted itself all up?" Cowboy asked from the murk.

"That's the one," Lynch said.

"*Shee-it,*" Cowboy said.

They were laagered-in in the Galena Mountains, between Valmy and Battle Mountain. They had gotten a preliminary report on the Guardians' goals and itinerary from the FSE late the previous afternoon, and had gotten a head start on the competition. They chose the Soda Springs-Truckee route, since it was the most direct one from Pineholm that wasn't liable to be totally impassable.

It had been a tough haul. As it had been last winter, here as everywhere else, snow had started early and started hard. Even the huge cleated tires of the Super Commando had been hard pressed to keep the car rolling through deep, dense drifts and over sheets of ice slick as greased glass. There'd been two occasions where they'd had to unship the cable from its spool beneath the angular snout, fasten it to a tree, and winch the vehicle over particularly treacherous patches. That was uncomfortable work, even for men like the Liberators— tricky, arduous, and dangerous—if the steel cable parted under the tension of ten metric tons, it could slice a man in half without slowing down. But they made it without mishap.

This morning they'd completed the crossing. And the figures dancing on the screen of Lynch's computer showed they were much closer to the Guardians' objective than the Guardians were.

"Ain't those boys gonna be surprised," Cowboy said and tittered.

CHAPTER
FIVE ——————————————————

The Guardians' route took them across Arizona
and New Mexico, then north along the Rio Grande
Valley to Colorado. They could have swung north
earlier and come in through Utah straight from the
west, but if they'd been reluctant to make a run at the
passes in the northern Sierra Madres, they were still less
thrilled about trying to tackle the dense blizzard-
wracked mountains of western Colorado.

As it was, Raton Pass, dead on the border between
New Mexico and Colorado, was no joy. But they made
it through the snowy pass, declining the offer of an old
codger with a beard like stiff wire to have his mule team
haul them over the pass for a mere three ounces of
silver. They drove north through a slate-colored afternoon with the snow-covered ramparts of the Sangre de
Cristo Mountains rising abruptly out of the Great Plains
just a few klicks to the left of them.

At Walsenburg, they turned and made a run at the
mountains. North La Veta Pass was supposedly
watched and kept clear by the city states (or village
states, anyway) of the Northern Rio Grande Valley Fed-

47

eration, the dominant power bloc in the San Luis Valley. To their surprise, the pass was open, with little snow on the ground, which was fortunate, since the pass showed no sign of life.

That was no surprise; the only occupation the NRGVF showed any enthusiasm for beyond general bloodshed was casting covetous eyes on the peaceful, prosperous, and remarkably well-defended settlement of Freehold. The Federation members were rapacious bastards who had joined readily with the mad Reverend Josiah Coffin's New Dispensation crusaders after a single defeat, lusting after the loot of Freehold.

It was deep dusk when the V-450 clattered past the few huddled lights of Alamosa and veered northwest toward Freehold.

"Seems strange to pass places where lights burn after dark, you know?" Casey commented wistfully as he nonchalantly steered the armored car along the relatively well-kept-up road.

"I know what you mean," Sam said from the ESO seat. "Especially after California."

The Effsees had enforced an early blackout wherever their law had run. It had been a lot more effective than most of their decrees, because nobody was anxious to attract the attention of FSE patrols after dark; few people would have burned their lights *without* the official blackout.

But, of course, it wasn't just California, and it wasn't just the Effsees. Road gypsy gangs terrorizing the highways in the few years preceding the War had made rural people cautious about showing light after dark. Since the One-Day War the gypsies had been joined by hordes of two-legged predators, ranging from fugitive mobs, hungry and ragged and all out of hope, to well-organized marauder bands. The homelike sight of a light in the night, all warm and comforting, was a beacon that drew human locusts as readily as moths.

So the citizens of Alamosa, who were protected by

their mountain ramparts, their own militia—mainly consisting of sheriff's deputies and state and local police—and occasional armed sweeps out of the Freehold itself, were showing an almost cocky confidence along with their lights.

"You know," Sam said, "somehow it's almost more lonely, seeing these little clusters of light amid so much emptiness."

McKay grunted from where he sat, "I like it lonely. Who needs the company of these pukes?"

The Guardians weren't loved by the NRGVF. The Federation still felt guilty about its quick switch of allegiances during the New Dispensation invasion. And a lot of households hereabouts tuned religiously—so to speak—to radio broadcasts emanating from Oklahoma City, the stronghold of Coffin's successor, former boy-wonder TV evangelist Nathan Bedford Forrest Smith. Denouncing the Guardians as personal agents of Satan was a major programming item on KFSU.

Nobody came out to challenge as they rolled across the valley, which aside from the substantial damage done by Coffin's crusaders had suffered little from the One-Day War and its aftermath. The Guardians were awfully well-armed agents of Satan, and a keen eye for the odds had always been a distinguishing characteristic of the NRGVF leadership.

They reached the slow slope leading to Freehold, which was a collection of homes sunk halfway into the earth for insulation, strung out for several klicks along the foothills of the San Juan range that formed the western boundary of the San Luis Valley.

"Still no answer," Sloan said from the ESO seat, shaking his head. "It's almost as if there's nobody home."

McKay peered out through the vision blocks. There were fields to either side of the two-lane asphalt road, winter bare and empty except for the occasional shack or mutant scarecrow shape of a windmill or a clump of Herefords huddled together for warmth. The land looked deceptively flat. Its apparent slow undulation concealed abrupt arroyos and steep low hills, which made cultivation tricky and offered large amounts of dead ground to cover troop movements—as the New Dispensation fanatics had found out to their sorrow.

"Too much of this communications-trouble shit going around," McKay remarked. "It's starting to make me nerv—"

A wink of light from the road ahead and to their left cut him off. A moment later he was slammed into the hull as Casey Wilson slewed the car broadside. Half a second after that he rebounded hard off the thin rubber matting laid over the steel deck plates as Casey shoved home the accelerator and Mobile One drove into the ditch, bucking and snorting like a horny dragon. Somewhere amid all this abuse his mind registered the hateful crack of a shaped-charge warhead exploding, muffled by distance and the hull.

"What's going on?" he heard Sam demanding as he rolled over, feeling as if he'd just been dragged down five flights of stairs on his right side.

"Antitank rocket, Sam," Tom Rogers said from the turret, sounding as calm as if he were giving him the time of day. The car reverberated to basso thunder and heeled way over to the left as Rogers cut loose a volley from the two big guns.

As soon as he'd seen the telltale flash, even as he was maneuvering the big car to evade the death bearing down on it, Casey had punched off the blackout headlights and turned on the infrared beams—a feat of co-ordination that wasn't too demanding for a former fighter ace, and the driver's console of Mobile One was nowhere near as elaborate as even the beautifully de-signed cockpit of the F-16 he was used to. He was driv-ing now by means of a television screen set under the driver's forward viewslit, which had come on auto-matically when he killed the headlights.

Forward blocks and screen alike flared. A blast buffeted the car as it jounced over the irregular landscape. "Jesus *Christ!*" Sloan exclaimed.

"Grenade launcher," Tom said casually.

"They must have passive IR tracking our beams," Casey said. Gone was the usual California mellow. In its place was a strangely cold and matter-of-fact voice. "Going to low-light mode."

He killed the infrared headlights. The image on the screen dimmed almost to blackness, then came back with a feeble, shadowy view of the terrain ahead. The computer-enhanced low-light television which had kicked in was a bona-fide miracle of modern science, something even Billy McKay could approve of. But not even a daredevil like Casey could be happy about trying to drive fast across broken terrain with just it to go by.

By dint of sheer will power, McKay was hauling himself upright. Rogers fired another blast from the .50-caliber gun and the automatic grenade launcher in the turret, and then the vehicle fishtailed left and right with a prim little ass-waggle and came to a stop.

"Dead ground, Billy," Casey said.

"Roger." McKay was already pulling his Maremont out of the clamps that held it to the hull. They had been working together so long that they functioned as a perfect team with a minimum of commands or even of communication. Casey knew what his commander wanted and had done it without being told.

"C'mon, Sloan," McKay said. "We're going for a walk."

He popped the hatch and dove out into the darkness. The cold hit him like a knife, stabbing deep into his lungs. An instant later Sloan hit the half-frozen dirt beside him. He'd been in motion as soon as McKay was, gathing up his Galil/M-203 combo, a Galil SAR like Rogers's with a single-shot 40-mm grenade launcher slung under the barrel. Casey wasn't the only one who knew his role to perfection. Together with McKay's lightweight M-60, the combo gave them a hell of a lot of firepower for a mere two men.

Sam raised himself up, grimacing slightly. As he always did when the car was under way, he'd been wearing a rip-stop vest with twelve little pouches, each carrying a round for the M-203, in case of emergencies just like this. Twelve little 1½-inch-thick cylinders—like miniature trash cans, the kind with the domed tops—were not very comfortable to land on.

"You go left," McKay's voice said over the com. "Me right."

They got up and moved out, hunched over like stooped old men. Casey had driven Mobile One into a depression just shallow enough to hide from the ambushers' view. They ran in opposite directions, McKay back toward the road, Sloan into the field, increasing their separation from one another and from the car to reduce the damage in case one of them was spotted.

An explosion sent dirt and light in a fountain forty meters beyond the V-450. Sloan recoiled as a frozen clod of earth grazed his nose, dropped to one knee, then drove on. His old gunnery-officer's instincts told him that their assailants were firing their grenade launcher blind. But his reflexive wince embarrassed him. *McKay wouldn't have ducked if the damned thing had bounced off that thick skull of his,* he thought ruefully.

Shouts and shots peppered the night somewhere off to his right. He had no idea what was going on, lacked data even to speculate. That the Freeholders were in some kind of trouble was a chilling near certainty, though.

He turned towards the sounds. He clambered up a meter-high embankment, worked his way to the top of a rise, moving the last few meters on his belly. The sky was clear and there was no moon, but it wouldn't be a good idea to let himself get silhouetted.

He eased up over the edge. He had a high-explosive, dual-purpose grenade up the spout of the M-203. It combined a shaped charge with fragmentation effect, giving him effective punch against lightly armored vehicles as well as infantry. The Galil had self-luminous tritium night sights. He peered across the eerie pale blobs toward the slumbering snow-clad bulk of the San Juans.

He saw a flash a hundred meters away. The crump of the shot reached him just before another grenade completed its slow-looping flight and blew another chunk out of nowhere behind them.

"McKay," he subvocalized, "I'm in position. I think I've spotted their grenadier. Do you see anything?"

"Roger that, Navy boy." McKay was lying on his belly with the Maremont's bipod down and the weapon stuck through some kind of dried-out bush that sprang right straight out of the ground without any kind of main stem. He was just a few meters from the ditch that ran along the road, ensconced on enough of a swelling in the uneven landscape to give him a decent view.

Whoever the opposition was, they weren't too bad. They moved in short rushes, kept low, and went to earth, and they were careful not to show too much outline against the pale backdrop of the mountains. They talked too much and tended to shoot at shadows, but so did just about all the troops McKay had ever gone up against, including the Effsees. They might have been regulars, or they might have been another of the innumerable bands of amateurs who'd picked up the principles of good soldiering by sheer brute natural selection in the harsh after-the-holocaust environment. McKay had seen plenty of those in the last year and a half.

But whoever they were, they weren't quite good enough. On the other hand, not much of anybody was good enough to take on the Guardians.

"I got 'em," he told Sloan. "Spotted about a dozen. Got a target?"

"Sure do."

McKay grinned. The proper military response was

"affirmative." But Sloan hated jargon.

Tom and Casey were being left conspicuously out of the conversation. They would keep Mobile One as a potent reserve, but there were weapons out in that bone-chilling Colorado night that could peel them open like a cellophane wrapper on a granola bar. The V-450 would stay out of the fight unless the shit came down disastrously on Sloan and McKay.

Fat fucking chance, McKay thought. "Rock and roll," he said.

He let Sam have the first shot—let the bad guys look that way first: Sloan could roll out to a new location easier than he could. But he didn't give the grenade a chance to land before he cut loose with a short aimed burst.

Even in the dark he could see his bullets kick up chunks of earth, and a scream came out of the hillside. Sloan's grenade went off; more screams, and lots of return fire winking like a dozen signaling lamps. Quickly, McKay traversed the muzzle a few degrees left to cover a flicker of muzzle flash, then fired another precise four rounds. Then he cut loose at the landscape in general, keeping the bursts short to reduce the chance of a failure to feed, but putting out a high-density fire while Sloan pounded the ambushers with grenades.

For an enemy armed with two or three full-auto weapons—M-16s, by the sound—and the rest semi-auto or bolt-action hunting guns, the firepower of the 40-mm launcher and the 7.62-mm machine gun had to be awesome, overwhelming. Had they been cool hands they could have concentrated fire on the enormous muzzle flash of McKay's MG and put him in a world of hurt. But he wasn't giving them a lot of time to think things out. The firefight was going down at close enough range that the nearest enemies could literally feel the muzzle blast of the Maremont puff against their faces like bolts of compressed air from the fat-barreled air guns McKay and his buddies had shot each other with as kids. Not the sort of thing to make you feel secure.

Battles aren't won by killing all your enemies. They're won when your enemy decides he's beaten. It didn't take long to convince the ambushers. In less than a minute McKay saw them slipping back up the road, keeping good order and firing often enough to keep their tormentors honest. He caught one who didn't stay low enough with a short burst that sent him spinning, entrails spilling out of him like sawdust stuffing. Then they were gone.

Silence settled in, heavy and strange after the terrible tumult of a moment before. McKay gave it several minutes. He heard nothing but the wind in the dry grass, and the moaning of a couple of injured men.

"Sam," he said at length, "shag ass back to the car and swap places with Tommy."

That was too much for the ex-naval officer's pride. "But—" he began.

"Belay it, sailor. There's some serious snooping and pooping to do. Now *move*."

Half an hour later, McKay and the former Green Beret were back.

"We heard shooting," Sloan said as Tom slipped into the darkened car. "Did you have any trouble?"

"Some wise asses thought they wanted to play hero," McKay said from the darkness. "We talked them out of it."

Rogers turned around to help McKay ease a burden off his shoulder onto the deck. McKay slipped inside and shut the door, and Casey, poised like a leopard at a water hole behind the wheel, keyed on red interior lights that would interfere as little as possible with his night vision.

Sloan continued to keep a lookout for trouble above. When McKay and Rogers had vanished into the darkness, Casey had pulled the vehicle forward about twenty meters, so that it was hull down behind the rise with only the turret exposed, to cover as much as possible of the surrounding countryside. That done, Casey had risked a quick trip outside to surround the car with sensors. Despite its armor and awesome armament, the armored car would be nothing more than an incredibly expensive death trap if hostile parties managed to sneak up on it—especially if they had antitank capability, as whoever had ambushed them all too evidently did.

What the two scouts had stretched out on the thin rubber mat was a slight-built man—boy, actually, couldn't have been more than seventeen—in jeans and a store-bought camouflage smock, the left shoulder of which was black with blood. He was unconscious but breathing strongly.

Casey glanced back. His shoulders jerked, and he did a double take. "Holy shit," he said, "that's Lanny Henderson!"

McKay and Rogers stared at each other across the injured youth. There was no mistaking the young black man who had been the first Freeholder McKay had ever seen, in Angie Connoly's house when he and Sloan were being nursed back to health after Josiah Coffin's elite Brotherhood of Mercy had staked them in the crater left by a ground-bursting twenty-five megatonner to die of irradiation.

Rogers frowned. He had already hyposprayed a jolt of painkiller into the kid's arm. Now he was sawing open the blood-soaked cammie smock to dress the wound.

"What's going on down there?" Sloan demanded.

McKay grimaced. "I wish to hell I knew."

Rogers was gently peeling away the cloth stuck to the kid's body by drying blood when his eyes came open. His thin body jackknifed on the deck, and his right hand clawed for McKay's eyes.

"Murderers!" the boy hissed as McKay ducked back and caught his wrist. "Murderers! *You killed Ruby!*"

CHAPTER
SIX ───────────────

For a long moment, McKay just sat there, feeling like he'd been shot in the gut. He wasn't aware of anything outside himself, not the cursing of the angry youth on the deck, nor the red glow of the car's interior, nor the smell of sweat and blood and motor oil.

Eventually it occurred to him that the steel decking was being pretty rough on his knees. He snapped back to reality.

Lanny Henderson was writhing furiously, like a rattler pinned by a forked stick. Rogers was doing his best to hold him down without further aggravating his wound. McKay stared down at the boy.

"What did you say?" he asked. His tongue felt thick like a pair of rolled sweat socks in his mouth.

The kid spat full in McKay's face.

People had done that before. Of course, they'd never looked quite the same after that. But McKay just pulled a handkerchief out of one of the many pockets of his coveralls and wiped the spittle off without so much as changing the odd expression frozen on his heavy face.

"What did you say?"

Furious eyes glared up at him. "You know what you did. Lemme up, goddam you!"

"No, son," Tom said. "No, we don't know. What are we supposed to have done?"

The kid pulled his head back against the deck and stared up at the older man, straining his eyes as if he could see right through to the center of him and see the truth. Then he squeezed his eyes tightly shut at the pain in his shoulder and his soul.

"No. This is crazy. You're trying to make me think—"

The first shock of impact had started to wear off for McKay, and he reacted the way he always did when something caught him off balance: He got mad.

"What are you trying to say, you miserable little son of a bitch?" he roared. He caught a handful of the smock and pulled the boy bodily off the deck, a huge fist cocked to strike.

In an instant, Tom Rogers was forcing himself between the two like a wedge. With the reflexes of a mongoose, Casey was at his side, grabbing McKay's fist.

For a heart-stopping moment, it looked as if there was going to be a battle to the finish right there on the red-lit deck of Mobile One. McKay combined enormous size and strength with the experience of somebody who'd been fighting anybody who looked at him with both eyes simultaneously since he was four years old. But Rogers had the solidity and unflinching tenacity of a badger, and Casey brought a total abandon to hand-to-hand combat that was so utterly unpredictable as to be lethal.

For a moment, McKay fought them with his muscles straining and the sweat standing out on his forehead despite the chill in the armored car. Then with the suddenness of an electron changing energy states, the madness went out of him.

Gently he lowered the wounded youth to the floor. The kid's dark face had gone pale, but he kept a defiant jut of his lower lip and a furious look in his eyes. The breath came out of McKay in a long, shuddering sigh.

"Sorry," he said, not looking at the kid or his comrades. "Something—it just set me off."

"What's going on?" Sloan asked for what McKay realized was about the eighteenth time. The kid's accusation had been the last thing he heard before a roaring rushed into his ears that blotted out everything else.

Rogers assured Sloan that nothing was happening, examining the injury for signs of fresh damage as he did so. There didn't seem to be any.

"Too many weird things happening," McKay said, half to himself. He felt strange. *A commander can't afford to blow up like that,* he thought. *Especially not if he's in charge of an elite team like this.*

With professional calm, Rogers dressed Lanny's wound while Casey eased himself back into the driver's seat. One of McKay's 7.62 rounds had busted the kid's collarbone but failed to tumble, and passed through without doing a whole lot of damage.

Glancing every now and then at his leader, Rogers coaxed the story out of the injured youth, who kept insisting that they should *know* what had gone down, because they were the ones who'd done it. But Rogers's quiet persistence wore him down.

Early this morning a neighbor had been passing Angie Connoly's house high up a hillside when she noticed the door standing open. She took her shotgun from the rack of her pickup and moved cautiously up to investigate. A glance inside and she'd run for help, pausing only to vomit next to the front porch. In ten minutes she was back with a dozen heavily armed Freeholders. The horror they'd found inside brought angry tears to young Henderson's eyes.

"It was awful," he said, shaking his head violently as if trying to throw the images out from behind his tightly shut eyes. "There was Lucy Zmed, and John Oakie, and—and Dr. Vasquez. All dead."

The Zmed girl was the daughter of a Freehold family whom Angie Connoly paid to keep house for her, as she had a busy schedule and no aptitude for housework. John Oakie was a computer systems-design specialist, a former business partner of Connoly's who still frequently worked with her. And Ruby Vasquez, the settlement's chief physician, was one of Angie's closest friends. She was an intensely social person who never liked to spend much time at home. And as perhaps the most popular person in the colony, she didn't have to. Freeholders frequently stayed in one another's homes, so it was easy to account for why all three had been there.

Which left one huge question mark glaring at them.

Suddenly, McKay and Rogers lifted their heads and turned to look at Casey. He was sprawled in his chair in his usual big-cat way, his eyes shifting ceaselessly back and forth between the viewslits and the low-light TV, keeping a constant lookout for movement in the night. But there was something in the curve of his body, in the way he drummed his fingers on the steering wheel, in the tautness of the skin around the eyes, which showed how intently he was focused on the young man's story.

Henderson had recalled once again that the people he was telling about the murders were the very ones who'd committed them, as far as he knew, and was lashing his head from side to side, cursing them half coherently and moaning something about *the others, the others*. The aftershocks of major trauma had his mind fogged.

McKay looked at Rogers. "Sedative?" he subvocalized. If the kid bashed his brains out on the steel deck, they weren't going to get much more out of him. And they were just getting to the important part.

Rogers shook his head. "Not after the anesthetic. Let me talk to him."

McKay waited while Rogers spoke to the kid, not saying much in particular, just soothing nonsense, the way he might gentle a frightened horse. Finally Lanny settled down again.

"It was terrible," he said faintly. "They'd been shot, cut, beaten—anything you could think of. And Dr. Chen said—said the women had been raped—"

McKay shut his eyes.

"What about Ms. Connoly?" Casey asked very quietly.

"She wasn't home. She was off in Gilpin, talking to Mayor Westlake about leasing some grazing land to the townspeople. She came back this morning. Mr. Oakie was over working on some problem for those people in California, that FSE thing. And Ruby—well, you know Ruby."

Casey said nothing. His hands gripped the steering wheel so fiercely his arms trembled.

McKay sat and stared at the cargo compartments built into the inner hull of Mobile One. His eyes looked right past them. He was seeing Ruby Vasquez on the ride down to Gilpin that first summer morning, sitting on a fold-down seat and hanging onto a strap for balance. She had worn a striped halter top and jeans and gunbelt, and had chattered away about the history of the Freehold in that bright, snappy way of hers, half sarcastic, half compassionate. He thought about her, and he thought about what Lanny Henderson had said, and he wanted to hurt someone more than he ever had in his life.

He just didn't know who. Not yet, but he'd find out.

Rogers was asking the youth about the *others* he had mentioned. "The Norrises," he said vaguely. "Lived up north, near the outskirts of the Freehold by the La Garita road. Killed them, too, all four of them—"

"What the fuck makes you think *we* did this?" McKay asked through clenched teeth. His voice sounded as if he'd been gargling with lye.

Tom laid a hand on his arm. "Billy."

McKay felt the rage boiling inside him again, but he knew he could control it now. The rage had a focus. And it wasn't this poor kid.

"The note." Lanny was drifting now from shock and the painkiller.

"What note?" McKay asked.

"The note you left." The kid spoke without rancor now. "Written in blood on some of Ms. Connoly's stationery. The one that said, you know, 'This is what happens to those who betray the Guardians.' "

The words hit like a harpoon, but it took some time for the meaning to seep out of them like slow poison.

"That's bullshit," McKay said at last. "How can you believe—"

"Movement, McKay," Sloan said from the one-man turret.

Lights glared into life on the ESO console. Buzzers farted in alarm.

"They're behind us, Billy," Casey said, scanning the readouts from the computer monitoring the scanners. "Forty meters—wait, they're in front of us, too."

"Christ, they're surrounding us," McKay said, "Casey—"

He was going to say, *get us out of here,* but Casey hit the gas and got them out of there, spilling McKay to the deck with jackrabbit acceleration.

"Sloan! What the fuck are you waiting for? *Fire 'em up!*" McKay bellowed as he slid hard into the engine housing.

"But they're friends!"

The car rocked to the explosion of a 40-mm grenade that filled the compartment with thunderous noise.

"They're tryin' to kill us," McKay roared.

Sloan didn't need any more urging. He depressed the muzzles of the turret guns and hit the switch that fired both electronically, traversing from left to right as he did so. A flaming curtain of explosions, HEDP interspersed with deadly white phosphorus, appeared thirty meters from the vehicle. Sloan didn't want to die because of some bizarre misunderstanding, but he didn't want to kill any of their allies if he could avoid it. He was trying to make them keep their heads down and throw off their aim.

Tom was still kneeling over the now semiconscious captive, as though the laws of physics had no more meaning for him that the confusion and anger boiling around inside his buddies.

Let ourselves get hypnotized by all this weird shit coming down, McKay thought as he retrieved his machine gun. *We let our emotions get involved, and it almost cost us our asses.*

Small-arms fire rattled like hail off the V-450's steel and titanium skin. McKay slid open the rear firing port and the shutter on the armored vision block above it, poked the M-60 into the night, and cut loose at the figures firing after the fleeing vehicle. He saw some go down, but couldn't really tell if he'd hit any of them or not. He had a lot less compunction about killing former friends than Sloan—in fact, he didn't have a lot of compunction about killing *anybody* who was trying to kill him—but he was mainly busting caps, trying to make the enemy pull their heads back into their shells and forget about shooting at them.

Mobile One was bucking like a steer beneath a rodeo rider as Casey hot-rodded across the broken landscape. The shadowy forms that had been slipping down in front of the vehicle to cut it off scattered as the huge car burst in among them, then fled in all directions as McKay sprayed them with bullets. Mobile One cut east and ran like a bunny.

Like a sly desert jackrabbit, to be exact. Casey darted in random zigs and zags, left and right to confuse the enemy's aim—he would have called it "jinking." Anti-tank rockets reached for them like blazing comet fingers; grenades ripped bright holes in the darkness.

Casey dodged them all, staying alive by intuition and sheer skill.

"How did they organize this?" Sloan demanded from the turret. This was obviously no blind blundering in the dark, but a skillfully coordinated attack, a pincers movement that had damned near trapped them in its jaws.

He was shooting for real now, friends or no friends. He'd seen what happened to armored-vehicle crews when their luck ran out: They turned into calcined black mummies, incinerated by blazing fuel.

"Our freek scanner would've picked it up if they'd used radios," Sloan persisted.

"Telephones," McKay said in disgust, slamming the feed tray cover on a fresh belt of 7.62 ammo. "Fuckers got telephones strung all over the place. Secure, reliable commo; no jive." During the siege by the New Dispensation, the Guardians had taught their Freeholder what they could about modern war. They had learned the lessons well.

We're gonna have to hit a cache for resupply, he thought as he burned up half the belt in bursts spaced so closely together they seemed continuous. They were scarfing ammo at a huge rate, and had kissed their sensors good-bye in the bargain, which McKay had mixed feelings about, but they'd helped save their asses this night.

The radio came to life.

"Guardians, this is Freehold," the voice of Angie Connolly said, crisp and dry as a judge pronouncing a sentence of death. "I don't know what made you come back here to revisit the scene of your crime. You got clean away, after leaving plenty of distinctive tire tracks, in case there were any doubts in our minds. In any event, our people will do their best to apprehend you. I doubt they'll succeed. They're amateurs, and you're very *professional* killers."

"Fuckin' bitch," McKay said, firing his MG.

"Angie, this is me, Casey. We've heard what happened here, and we had nothing to do with any of it. You have to believe—"

"I wish I could. You're what disappoints me most, Casey." Her voice caught. She paused, then went on, "I had always thought it was too pat a generalization, but I guess this shows that militarism really does drive people crazy. You're mad dogs, Casey. I tears me apart to say it. But it's true."

CHAPTER
SEVEN ──────────────────

Once out of range of the Freehold attackers, the Guardians stopped and left Lanny Henderson by the side of the road, wrapped in a blanket. They stuck a flare in the ground next to him and set it off, just to make sure he wasn't missed. They didn't think it would be long before he was picked up. Angie Connoly's vindictive words had made it clear the Freeholders intended to pursue them to the best of their ability.

"Who could believe shit like this?" he demanded. "I knew this fucking Connoly bitch was crazy, but I never realized she was stupid."

He knew the words hurt Casey, who loved Angie Connoly. That was why he said them. He needed something to lash out at. Angie had added to his fury and confusion, with her anger and her certainty and her self-righteousness, but she wasn't here. Striking at her through Casey somehow made sense to him, in the mood he was in.

"It's all too easy for them to believe it," Sam said grimly. "We've been personal friends with a lot of the Freeholders, but politically they don't have much sympathy with us. And they have what must look like pretty compelling evidence.''

"Their evidence is shit," McKay said. "Somebody knocks over the first house they come to in the Freehold, then tortures the people into telling them where Angie Connoly lives. Then they sign our name to their little note. Now how the fuck compelling is that? It's—it's—ah, damn, what's the word I want?''

"Transparent," Sloan said.

"Yeah. Transparent. See? Nobody could buy it.''

"Billy," Tom said. "When something like this happens to your friends and neighbors, you don't think about it too clearly.''

McKay sighed. "Yeah, Tom. You're right. You're always right.''

He took a cigar from his breast pocket and unwrapped it. It was broken in half from when he'd hit the dirt earlier. He stuck half into his mouth and struck a match before realizing he was forbidden to smoke in the vehicle.

"Son of a bitch," he said, putting the match out with a savage shake.

They took sporadic fire all the way across the valley.

"The NRGVF must be taking a hand," Sloan said from the ESO seat as gunfire flashed from a darkened orchard to the right of the road. Bullets clattered off the hull, harmless as so many handfuls of thrown gravel.

"You sure, Sam?" Casey asked. "They've never been too friendly to the Freehold. Why would they risk their necks for them?''

"It ain't that they're friendly to *them*. It's that they hate *us*, 'cause we know what chickenshits they turned out to be," McKay said.

"There sure aren't enough Freeholders to be giving us this much grief," Sloan said, wincing as a high-powered rifle bullet clanged off the hull right beside his right ear. The foamed middle layer of the sandwich armor resisted spalling—the kinetic energy of high-velocity strikes could knock chunks of metal off the inside of an armored vehicle, like a cue ball striking a billiard ball. Conventional small arms couldn't do much to Mobile One.

"I never thought the Northern Rio Grande people had this much guts," Sam admitted.

The big turret guns were thudding, a sound like two giant typewriters going at once. White flashes of explosion danced among the trees. The strobe effect caught figures running away as fast as they could in a series of freeze-frames.

"Not too brave," McKay grunted.

Glowing like a meteor, a Molotov cocktail arced out of the trees and down toward the road. Rogers's .50-caliber gun splintered a tree and a would-be firebomber who thought he was hidden behind it. The cocktail landed in the ditch and went out.

"*Some* of 'em are brave," McKay amended, "but they ain't smart."

They backtracked past Alamosa, headed for the southern pass through the Sangre de Cristo Mountains.

U.S. 160 through the Sangres was a basic mountain road, none too wide, with plenty of switchbacks and places where the tall Ponderosa pines crowded the road. Ideal ambush country, in other words. Mobile One went up it as fast as Casey could goose it. The way the Guardians saw it, if they took the road slow and cautious, that just gave any bad guys a better shot at them. And with any kind of speed at all, ten metric tons gave them plenty of bargaining power.

But there was nothing. They drove past a dozen perfect ambush spots with their hearts in their throats and the engine laboring. But nobody lifted a finger to stop them.

"Maybe they decided that they'd done their part," McKay remarked. "They don't like the Freeholders that much. And they ain't never struck me as any too eager to die."

Ten minutes later they approached the pass itself. Sloan was playing with his ESO board, fiddling with the instrument and the hull-mounted sensors.

"Get a load of this," he said, frowning and holding a lightweight headset to one ear. "Funny sound, coming from up ahead."

"Put it on the speakers," McKay said.

The cabin filled with a whining growl, which seemed to build in short jerks, then crescendoed in a high-pitched roar. The rhythm reminded McKay of the grunting and groaning you heard in fuck flicks: *I'm gonna come/I'm going come/I'm gonna co-o-ome!*

"Chain saws," he said. "Jesus Christ."

"Dropping trees in our path," Tom said from the turret.

In another minute they came around the bend and there it was. The road unwound into a fairly straight path with a valley spilling out to the right of it and a ridge shouldering in close to the left. Where the ridge came closest to the road, a tree was just toppling over with slow-motion grace, to join several already lying across the pavement.

The Guardians had no trouble discerning this, because there were at least a dozen jeeps and pickups parked by the side of the road, and a giant mob of good old boys in hunting vests and caps with furry flaps pulled down over their ears, all milling around with guns on their shoulders, slapping asses and smoking and joking and lining up at the tailgate of a Blazer where there was a big keg of cocoa or beer or some damn thing. Half of the vehicles had their headlights on. There were kerosene lanterns glowing everywhere, and a bunch of torches burning merrily, stuck in the ground or being waved around endangering everybody's health.

Casey burst out laughing. "These folks sure know how to run an ambush, man!"

"Peasants with torches," Sam said, shaking his head.

"What, they think we're the bride of fucking Frankenstein?" McKay said.

Casey stopped the V-450 fifty meters away from the extraordinary assemblage. The turret turned, guns pointing like the sensitive snout of some giant beast. The longer barrel rose, fell, and hunted around a little with little furtive servomotor whirs. Then it emitted two loud bangs and a flame about the size of a Subaru.

The tailgate keg flew apart in a spray of sticky hot gray-brown fluid. Scalded manhunters ran in all directions, squalling like frightened calves. When everybody was well away from the commissary wagon, Rogers gave it another burst of .50-caliber shot and a single round of HEDP.

It went up like a NASA Titan II blowing on the pad.

"Now that they know we're here," McKay said around the unlit stub of cigar he'd stuck into his mouth, "let's get a move on."

The V-450 rumbled into life. It moved with deceptive slowness at first, gathering speed gradually but inexorably despite the grade. When it hit the first of the trees it was moving at a good fifty klicks an hour.

The pine tree caught under the angle of its snout and was pushed along before the vehicle with a screeching sound of limbs on pavement. It hit the next tree, and they were both bulldozed along into a third.

The fourth and final tree was stuck in somehow, refusing to budge. For a moment Mobile One's engine strained while about a hundred hopeful eyes watched from prairie dog level, out on the flat. Then the flange-like cleats on the tires caught, and the giant armored car rode right up onto the trees and drove across them with much splintering and crashing and broken limbs spinning through the air.

When they came down the other side they saw what the pine boughs had hidden from view before: a couple of Alamosa County sheriff's cars, out of their bailiwick and parked nose to nose across the road. A couple of uniformed deputies crouched behind them, hopefully aiming shotguns.

"Right," McKay said, "Drive on, Casey."

The big car fishtailed once on broken limbs and squashed needles, then laid rubber. One deputy fired two quick blasts and then joined his buddy in trying for the land speed record. Mobile One hit the juncture of the two cars and never slowed down.

Sam Sloan looked to the side where one cruiser was sort of corkscrewing across the valley, hitting its nose and rear bumper, to land with a splash on its roof in a small stream.

"We could have gone around the cars and the trees," he said.

"Yeah," McKay said. "But this way was so box office."

And they drove across the pass, leaving the intrepid militia of the Northern Rio Grande Valley Federation to pick themselves out of the landscape and beat out the grass fires their fallen torches had started with their camouflaged hunting jackets.

"You think it's gonna work?" Cowboy asked as he stepped out onto the front steps with a tocking of boot heels. The Liberators were making an early morning pit stop in southern Wyoming, at an honest-to-goodness post-holocaust general store, a cramped cinderblock oblong painted bright yellow long gone dingy, to get the lay of the land. Condensation puffed from Cowboy's mouth like dragon's breath as he took a bite from his candy bar.

The armored car was parked in front of the building, the long barrel of its 20-mm automatic cannon sticking out over its front glacis like the proboscis of a giant insect. Sitting on the step, drawing precise patterns in the gravel with a stick, Corbin looked up at him in irritation. "What's not going to work? And how can you bring yourself to eat that rubbish?"

"Contains one of the four basic food groups," Cowboy replied, chewing with his mouth open and treating the former SAS man to a good view of a brown-stained slab of tongue. "Chocolate."

The Australian shook his head in disgust.

The plan was Pirelli's.

Pirelli was a devout disciple of Carlos Marighela, a Brazilian revolutionary theorist who had evolved a scheme for the growth of world socialism through terror. Marighela believed that it was the liberal, democratic governments that needed fighting against, because truly repressive regimes would fall on their own. His plan was to use an ever-escalating campaign of terror to force liberal governments to more and more desperate means in an attempt to control the violence, until they finally threw aside any pretense of legality and resorted to out-and-out police state methods to quell the attacks. Then the people would rise and overthrow the state. Or so Marighela believed.

The first part of the program worked just fine. In various countries reasonably liberal regimes had been driven from power by Marighelaist terror campaigns, and replaced by oppressors every bit as hateful as Marighela had predicted they would be.

But then the oppressors perversely refused to be dislodged. By the One-Day War, the only state to rid itself of a brutal rightist government installed in response to Marighela's grand strategy was Argentina, and that nation only managed it because the junta picked a fight it couldn't win with Great Britain over the *Islas Malvinas*. Beyond that, the Marighelaists had over the long haul done a lot more to promote the spread of fascism than Adolf Hitler ever did.

Of course, mundane details of this nature did not discourage the truly committed, of whom Pirelli was proudly one.

No matter what minor quibbles could be raised with Marighelaism, its proponents tended to be expert in destruction, skilled in the arts of spreading confusion and fear—of terrorism, if you will. As a member of Italy's resilient Red Brigades, Pirelli had displayed a natural talent not just for the physical side of terror—shooting policemen or spraying acid in the faces of newspaper editors—but for the psychological side as well. For choosing the proper atrocities, and staging them in the most theatrical way possible, in order to achieve the most salutary effect.

It was a skill he'd put to good use with the Liberators in Europe. His plans for demoralizing insurgents in Amsterdam and Paris had worked flawlessly, and his scheme for destroying the underground in Barcelona a cynical masterpiece. *The Master of Disaster* was what Peter Lynch called him, with his tongue only partly in his cheek.

And now he had put every ounce of his artist's soul into creating his masterwork: the destruction of the Guardians.

"Here, now, do I hear the sounds of pessimism?" Peter Lynch asked, stepping out into the cold morning air. "Our plan *is* working. We have no need of conjecture on that score. The Guardians themselves have told us just how much confusion our little surgical action has thrown them into." He jutted out his chin and took a deep breath. "Ah, I love the smell of victory in the morning. It smells like napalm. Or whatever it was Robert Duvall said in that ridiculous movie."

"Ha, ha," Corbin said. "Very bloody funny."

Hands on hips, Lynch looked down at him. "Well, we're well socialized this morning, aren't we?"

"Bugger off."

"Ah, but that's more your speed than mine, isn't it, old chap?"

Corbin jumped to his feet, his face twisted in anger.

Van Thyssel emerged from the store, his head down between his solid shoulders, deep in conversation with Luttwak.

"Really, sir," Corbin said, confronting them, "I insist that you tell those men to stay off my back."

Van Thyssel sighed. "Have you been tormenting Reid again?"

Peter Lynch stared off at a distant range of mountains. Cowboy gnawed his candy.

Luttwak slapped Corbin on the shoulder. "Don't worry, my boy. They wouldn't tease you if they didn't like you, *nicht wahr?*"

Cowboy belched loudly.

"He was saying the plan wouldn't work," Corbin said, pointing accusingly at the mountainous demolitions expert.

Luttwak turned to him, his single dark eyebrow collapsed in on itself in the center. "Spreading defeatism, are we, Cowboy?" he asked, half heartily humorous, half ominously.

"Hey, now, partner. I can say what I want without worryin' about some little brown-nose trottin' off to the secret po-lice, because, shoot, we *are* the secret po-lice. And, anyway, I din't say that. I only asked if Miss Muffet here thought the plan was gonna work."

"Of course it will," Peter said, rubbing his hands together. "Our man Pirelli's a curious little chap, but he has the spark of genius. Things have gone swimmingly so far. We've totally cut the Guardians off from their tap into our communications. Everything else will fall into place like so many pieces of a jigsaw puzzle."

Van Thyssel frowned. "They have already deduced our existence," he said. He spoke slowly as he always did. His accent was thick but readily understandable. "Might that knowledge not . . . not lead them to counteract us, I believe you might say?"

"You personally approved the plan," Luttwak said.

"They haven't 'deduced our existence,' " Peter said.

"If you'll forgive my presumption in pointing it out, sir, they have grasped the readily apparent fact that someone's struck at them twice. It's quite a quantum leap from that to inferring *us*."

"It's not like they ain't made 'em some enemies along the way," Cowboy said.

"Precisely," said Lynch. He grinned engagingly. "Besides, they're unlikely to have the leisure to go hunting mysterious antagonists. *Trust* me."

As if on cue, Pirelli leaned out the hatch of the V-450. "Something I have."

They walked over to the car, their boots scrunching gravel with little bat squeaks.

The sky was high and the dirty white of spoiled milk. "This ain't just coincidence," Billy McKay said, squinting up into the cloud cover. "Somebody didn't just *happen* to wipe out Vista Systems three days before somebody just *happened* to trash our best friends in the Freehold—and tried to make it look like we did it, to boot."

"We are looking into the matter." Dr. Marguerite Connoly's words came back clear and cold as the Rocky Mountain air along the satellite link. It was funny how much she sounded like her daughter did when she was pissed off. Of course, Connoly senior was pissed off most of the time.

"But don't you think it's maybe a bit disturbing that we've just lost our tie-in to the entire Effsee communications net? The one asset that enabled us to stay afloat through the occupation?"

"I assure you, that is being investigated," she said. "In the meantime, these untoward events only increase the urgency of your mission."

"Jesus, it's just a *factory*. These were friends of ours. This is somebody taking direct action against us. And we're the ones on the ground, not some *investigators* in D.C."

"Guardian McKay, let me remind you that more than sixteen months have gone by since the One-Day War. In that time scarcely any of the components of the Blueprint for Renewal have been successfully recovered."

"Now, listen, at Heartland we—"

"Please do not interrupt me, Lieutenant. I'm perfectly aware that you assembled Blueprint resources at Heartland. They were then scattered, destroyed, or fell into the hands of the Federated States of Europe. I said *successfully* recovered. In all this time, New Eden and Project Starshine are the only facilities of any consequence which have been reclaimed, and neither has as yet made any substantive contribution to the rebuilding of America."

"A few little things got in the way," Sam Sloan murmured, "like an Effsee invasion." His throat mike wasn't tied into the long-distance link, of course.

"The United States lie prostrate, Lieutenant McKay. It is of the greatest urgency to restore well-regulated production of essential goods and services. The rapid recovery of all possible Blueprint resources is imperative. You must find this factory as quickly as possible; whatever it produces must be vital to America's regeneration. Unless you feel your personal concerns are more pressing, Lieutenant?"

McKay frowned so hard that it looked as if his face would cave in. *It was your daughter they tried to off, bitch.* "No, ma'am."

"You are to press on with your mission at all costs. You are not to waste time and energy chasing specters. If necessary, I'm sure the President will back me up on this 100 percent, busy though he is."

Because you've got him wrapped around your goddam little finger. "That won't be necessary, ma'am."

"In the meantime, rest assured our investigators will scrutinize every aspect of the irregularities which have arisen in the course of your current mission, Lieutenant."

Something in her tone made the short hairs of his nape rise. "You don't think we had anything to do with this Freehold thing?" he demanded.

"The Guardians' personal affairs are a matter of complete indifference to me," she said. "Washington, out."

"See? What did I tell you?" Peter Lynch asked with what on less refined features would have been a shit-eating grin. "They know there's something amiss, but they're powerless to do anything about it. Now all that remains is to lurk in the background while the Guardians do our work for us, and then—" He drew a painstakingly manicured finger across his throat.

Van Thyssel fingered his chin. "Hard to believe that it will be that simple."

"Sir, it *is* simple. It has the simple inevitability of a Greek tragedy. And even if they realize perfectly well what's happening, there is not one single solitary thing they can do about it. That's the beauty of the scheme."

"You sound like you've been hitting the coke, and the sun ain't hardly up," Cowboy said.

Peter shot him an angry look. "Don't tell me you're afraid of these Guardians," sneered Corbin.

"Why, I surely am," Cowboy said. He enfolded the juncture of the Australian's neck and shoulder in one gigantic hand. "I'm afraid for your sake, son. 'Cause when these here Guardians get ahold of you, they're gonna lay your ass out stiff as a wet cat in a Panhandle blizzard."

"What about you, my boisterous friend?" Luttwak asked.

"I ain't worried." He giggled and jiggled. "They can't hurt me. I'm the Cowboy."

CHAPTER
EIGHT ──────────────────────

"We have little to report about the tragedy at Pineholm," Morgenstern said. "Only that it appears to have been quite professionally executed."

"That's a pretty cold-blooded way to talk about the murder of a bunch of kids, Doctor," Sloan said.

"I am merely trying to appraise the situation objectively, Commander," Morgenstern said testily. "I suspect it to be a more reliable means of tracking down the perpetrators than emotionalism."

It was the second day after the flight from Freehold. Picking their way gingerly around Denver—still an enemy stronghold—the Guardians had reached the Colorado/Wyoming border and were about to enter the huge region they had to search.

"That won't bring them back, Doctor," Sloan said in a ragged voice.

"No. But it might prevent a recurrence. Rather more to the point, it might save your lives. Has it not occurred to you that both Vista Systems and the Freehold massacre were directed against you?"

"No kidding, Doc," McKay said. "But there ain't

nothing we can do about it. We've been forbidden to waste time hunting specters.''

Morgenstern sighed. ''We shall do what investigation we can and attempt to turn up information that might be of use. In the meantime, gentlemen, I advise you to stay alert.''

''Always, Doc,'' McKay said. ''Always.''

The old man sat on the porch in an ancient swing. ''You boys're lookin' for a factory, right?'' he asked.

Sam Sloan nodded encouragingly. ''That's right, sir.''

The ceaseless wind whistled up under the eaves of the peeling pitched-roof house set out in the midst of a vast bowlful of nothing called the Great Divide Basin, a 150-by-90-kilometer dent in Wyoming, which had the distinction that it split the otherwise continuous Continental Divide, which ran around both sides of it like a stream flowing around a rock. The wind whistled up under the hem of Sam Sloan's heavy coat, and down inside the turned-up collar. The old man's house was the only thing for klicks. How he lived was a mystery.

The codger swung some more, squinting out at his big empty domain from a face that looked like a miniature map of the area, with wrinkles here and bumps there. He had a hunting cap with fur-lined earflaps pulled down and tied in place by a piece of string that circumnavigated his head from crown to chin. His hands were jammed deep inside the pockets of a frayed plaid coat.

''Blanche and I used to sit out here on this swing in the evening,'' he said to nobody in particular, ''before she was taken to the Lord. That was years and years before the War. Years and years.''

He looked at Sam with a crow-bright eye. ''An' you don't know the name of this here factory.''

''That's correct, sir.''

''An' you don't know what this factory does?''

''No, sir.''

The old man laughed so hard that the rusty chains of the porch swing jingled like loose change, and the upper plate of his sadly yellowed dentures came loose so that his teeth shut while his mouth stayed open, which produced a pretty startling effect. Nothing daunted, he shoved the dentures out of his mouth with a grayish tongue, wrapped them in a handkerchief, and tucked them into a pocket of his coat.

He looked up at Sloan, his eyes bright and his upper lip drooping, which gave him an owlish appearance. "Sure do wish you boys the best of luck findin' it," he lisped. His cackling laughter followed them to the vehicle.

"Doin' a hell of a job winning hearts and minds there, Sloan," McKay said sourly when they'd clambered back into the relative warmth of the car. "Gave that old fart the best laugh he's had since World War II."

"Would you like to go back and beat him up, McKay?"

"It's early," Tom Rogers said in his best placid oil-on-water voice. "Give it time."

"Maggie Connoly sure ain't givin' us much time," McKay said.

Tom shrugged. That was all you could say about Maggie.

A plume of khaki dust crawled across an upside-down landscape. The image shimmered with atmospheric distortion.

"They're leaving the house," Peter Lynch reported. "Why in God's name did we have to get a reflecting telescope? This inverted image makes my head ache."

"It was the highest power and best quality available," said Luttwak, his usual secret policeman's self-confidence slipping a few millimeters out of place.

Cowboy guffawed. "You just wanna do some stargazing in between times."

Luttwak scowled.

For keeping tabs on the Guardians while minimizing the risk of being spotted themselves, Peter Lynch had decided they needed a telescope. Van Thyssel had been dubious, claiming they could keep more than adequate track of their quarry by monitoring their communications and shadowing them outside visual range. In agreement for once, Corbin and Cowboy sided with Lynch, saying they needed to maintain as much visual surveillance as they could. Those two had the most experience in special forces work, so Van Thyssel, who had served in a Dutch infantry unit before being transferred to military intelligence several years before the War, bowed to their judgment.

Since the avid amateur-astronomer Luttwak was the closest to being an expert on optics the Liberators boasted, they'd taken his advice as to what kind of telescope to liberate from the ruins of a giant shopping mall in the south Denver suburb of Englewood. Unfortunately, before they'd had a chance to examine the instrument, a large armed patrol from what had once been the Denver Federal Center in Lakewood came snooping around.

The DFC was held by the last remnants of the scattered crusading army of Josiah Coffin's Church of the New Dispensation, now under the control of Forrie Smith, and nominally allied to the FSE. But the Liberators were under strict orders never to acknowledge their connection to Maximov's empire, and besides, they felt the Children of the New Dispensation were too crazy to deal with anyway.

The quick-firing cannon mounted in the V-450's turret had made short work of the former Wells Fargo armored car leading the patrol, torching two trucks before most of the occupants could bale out. The Liberators' superior fire had routed the badly shaken survivors, and Corbin sniped a few down as they dodged through the ruins along Hampden Avenue just to keep their minds right. But the frequency scanner in the Super Commando intercepted traffic indicating a larger force was moving to the rescue, so the Liberators withdrew, carrying their prize.

It turned out to be an astronomical telescope with a 3.5-inch mirror, which, while of excellent quality, inverted the image of what you were looking at.

Lynch straightened. "Well, we're stuck with it. Let's pack it up and follow our friends."

"They're fools to stop here," Pirelli sneered. "What makes them think they can find their precious factory by questioning old men in the middle of nowhere?"

"Have you a better plan?" Luttwak asked. "They are being thorough. It is always best, thoroughness."

"Well," said Peter, "I for one certainly hope they don't intend to question the inhabitants of every isolated hovel between here and Saskatchewan."

"It's a cement plant," Billy McKay said.

Mobile One was parked on the verge of a highway in the Big Horn Mountains. McKay and Sam Sloan were standing next to the big car, looking at a collection of giant slab-sided buildings and dull steel hoppers nestled in the hollowed-out flank of a hillside four hundred meters away.

"We can't be sure," Sam said. "We ought to check it out."

"What's to check out? You think if we find the secret latch, the whole thing's gonna slide to one side and unveil a top-secret underground ICBM factory? It's a cement plant."

"Our informant said it was worth checking out," Sloan said stubbornly.

"Your informant was hoping to keep you buying rounds of drinks. He'd have told you there was a colony of naked sex nymphs living out here, if he thought it woulda got him another shot of Taos Lightning."

"Would you have picked Wolf Bayou for the world's

first functional fusion reactor from looking at the sur-face?'' Sloan asked.

McKay rubbed his jaw. "So what are we waiting for? Let's check it out."

"It's a bust," Billy McKay said.

"You can't be so easily discouraged," Dr. Morgen-stern's voice came back after a short relay delay. "No one said your assignment would be easy."

"No one told us our assignment was gonna be tramp-ing all over the hills and deserts in snow up to our asses, looking for some factory nobody even knows what does. What we volunteered for was to protect the Presi-dent in the event of nuclear war."

A pause, alive with static. "You could resign."

"Aw, hell. We can't do that. But, dammit, we've got no clues, we've got no information, and we've got Mag-gie Connoly crawlin' up our assholes each and every morning. In one week we have investigated five micro-wave-relay stations, one seismic-monitoring facility, one gutted-out ELF-monitoring station. We've been to one cement plant—" He favored Sloan with a dirty look. "—three electronic-component plants, a Toyota assembly plant the unions shut down before the War, and a tennis-shoe factory."

"I do wish I'd been able to see the look on my col-league's face when you told her why you thought that was the missing Blueprint facility," Morgenstern said drily.

McKay grinned. The plant had been filled with thou-sands of precut lasts and soles. McKay had assured them that it must be part of the Blueprint, awaiting only the arrival of fifteen thousand boat people to assemble the pieces and provide sneakers to a shoeless America. The doctor had not been amused.

"Plus we've been shot at by miners in the Gas Hills Uranium Mining District," McKay finished his recita-tion. "It has not been a real profitable search, Doctor."

They had developed a tendency to touch bases with Morgenstern on a regular basis. The elderly Israeli was a kind of touchstone to them, whose good sense and air of personal authority reassured them. They never acknowledged the fact; they were supposed to be self-reliant, the ultimate autonomous team. They were not supposed to need their little hands held. But they were not getting a lot of aid and comfort from Washington, and what they did get left them feeling demoralized and uncertain.

For his part, Morgenstern seemed secretly delighted that they were seeking his guidance, though he made a lot of growling noises about how busy he was. What he and the Guardians had to offer each other was respect. The same could not be said for Marguerite Connoly.

"Sir," Sloan said, "our usual method has been to settle into the search area and work with the local people, hunting for clues as to the location of our objective. But this time we have too much ground to cover."

"I understand," Morgenstern said. "Unfortunately, there's nothing I can do."

"If only Vista—" Casey began, then stopped.

"Yeah," McKay said. "They might be able to tap into the Effsee computers and see what they knew."

After the invasion of Heartland, Trajan's Expeditionary Force technicians had transcribed files containing all the information that had been gathered on the Blueprint for Renewal from the underground stronghold's database to FSE computers. The files had been locked, but given considerable time and resources the FSE had begun to decipher them. That meant Maximov now knew more about the Blueprint than anyone else.

The Guardians' allies at Vista Systems hadn't yet managed to penetrate the security surrounding the stolen Blueprint files that had been deciphered, but if the Effsees talked about any of their discoveries, or started to act on them, they knew about it. It was just such a discovery by FSE analysts that started the Guardians in search of Project Starshine in the bayou country of Louisiana. Now that asset was lost forever.

"Or the Freehold," Sam said. "God, how I wish we knew what happened there."

"No more than I, Commander. And, of course, Freehold isn't proving cooperative in our efforts to obtain more information. We know there were several individuals involved in the attack in California. It still seems apparent that the same group was responsible for the Colorado incident, though, of course, we have no direct evidence in support of such a supposition."

"We ain't seen any sign of them," McKay said.

"That disturbs me," Morgenstern said. "Then again, we may be reading too much into simple coincidence. New Eden out."

McKay leaned for a moment against Mobile One, listening to the coyotes sing a grossly swollen moon down into the Laramies. The mountains looked like chunks of silver in the moonlight. The cold seeped into his back and into each rib individually, making him think of those science demonstrations he'd done back in grade school where he'd stuck a leaf into colored water and showed how the dye was drawn up along the veins. The cold was doing that to his ribs.

On the other side of the vehicle, the hatch opened and slammed shut. Sloan came crunching around the prow of the car with the hood of his parka pulled up.

"Jesus, you're quiet," McKay said.

Sam grinned. "You always warn me not to pussyfoot up on you or you might blow my head off. So I stomp. Anyway, it's my turn in the barrel."

McKay handed the Galil/M-203 combo off to him. Even Iron Man McKay wasn't crazy about the idea of toting almost ten kilograms of Maremont's allegedly lightweight model of the M-60 through his whole watch. He was not the sort to sling a weapon while on watch, and all that iron weighed your arms down after a while.

Sloan's weapon was a pretty good compromise between portability and firepower, and they'd taken to passing it around on sentry duty.

At the sound of the vehicle's hatch, the coyotes had shut up. Now they started again, undaunted by the low conversation.

"Bold sons of bitches," McKay said.

"Gotten more that way since the War," Sam said, gazing thoughtfully across landscape whited out by snow and moonlight. "Maybe they reckon man's stepped aside to let them take over."

A single wail rose up, seemingly out of the mountains, peaked, then diminished among yaps.

"Eerie fucking sound," McKay said.

"Lonely."

"Don't they hibernate or anything? It's *cold.*"

"What fur was invented for, McKay."

McKay showed him where the clacker for the Claymores was hung off the hull, then handed over the special night glasses with the starlight and IR capability and the fancy microprocessors. They stood for a while.

"Guess I better take a turn around the perimeter," Sloan said. "What are you doing still out here? Figure the warmth of my company will banish the cold?"

"Fat chance," McKay said. But he still didn't move.

"Well?" Sloan urged.

"Well, hell. I'm bugged."

"What about?"

"This whole Vista-Freehold thing. I mean, maybe it was just random crazies. Except the Vista thing was professional, Doc M. says, and this Freehold thing was pulled off pretty slick, too. I mean, they pretty much had to be connected, since those were our two links to the FSE."

"I agree. In spite of what Washington likes to believe."

"So why did they try to make it look like we did the Freehold thing?"

"Who knows? A grace note, maybe. They taught us in Guardians' training to do what we could to mess up the enemy on general principles." Sloan got a rueful expression that might have been taken for a smile at a distance. "They've done a fine job of that, you have to admit."

"So what's eating me is, who are these dudes? And why haven't we seen any more sign of them?"

Sloan shrugged. "Maybe Effsees who missed the boat. Maybe some of Forrie Smith's people. He has a lot of friends."

"And we got a lot of enemies. But I mean, if these dudes are after us, why haven't they made a play for us? Why haven't they tried an ambush or something?"

"Maybe they're smart."

McKay stared at him without comprehension.

"I mean, we are the Guardians, McKay. We've beaten Maximov's first team—Vesensky—and even the Expeditionary Force came off second best just about every time they tangled with us. Maybe they just wanted to rescue their communications and take some reprisals without directly messing with us."

"You're saying they're afraid of us?"

"Yes. That's about it. Why shouldn't they be?"

McKay just shook his head and went to bed.

CHAPTER
NINE

For two weeks they chased the phantom factory through western Wyoming and the Dakotas.

"We're just hitting the high points," Sloan remarked wryly. "There must be fifteen thousand factories in this region that *might* be the one we're looking for."

"And Maggie's gonna make us go back and search every one, if we don't find it on this first sweep," McKay said sourly.

In fact, Sam had summed it up quite well. The Guardians were making a quick preliminary pass over the assigned area, looking for any clues they could find, asking survivors—the ranchers and the shopkeepers and the lumbermen and traders—if they knew of any mysterious facilities. They were trying to establish a rough familiarity with the region, a kind of intuitive foundation for the search.

That was their rationale. What they really wanted was to stumble across someone who'd say, "Oh, that? I know just the place," and lead them to the unknown facility.

It showed no sign of happening.

Washington was going nuts. Perhaps because Connoly realized the futility of her demands, she was getting shriller every day, urging the Guardians to produce results.

In the grind of a long, fruitless, and quite possibly hopeless search, memories of the slaughter of Vista Systems and in the Freehold began to melt into the high-volume background noise from Washington. The possibility of some group specifically acting to counter the Guardians faded in their minds as no action was taken against them beyond the occasional minor shooting scrape along the way.

"Montana."

"Say again, Washington," Billy McKay said, frowning at the cargo compartments set into the V-450's hull. They were rattling along an awful state road that carried them north of the devastation of Minot under obscenely cheery blue skies heaped high with ice-cream clouds.

"Montana," said the anonymous female voice. In fact, the Guardians knew it belonged to one of Connoly's technical advisers. She just *sounded* anonymous. "We have collated further data and are presently able to refine your search parameters."

Sam pursed his lips and shook his fingers, impressed by this bravura display of bureaucratese.

"You're sure of this now?" McKay asked in a voice thick with sarcasm.

"We have verified these adjustments to our original operational assumptions to a high order of probability."

"Right. Montana. It's been *three weeks,* Washington. That's how long we've spent chasing all over the goddam north central states. Now you say Montana to us."

"We have a severely disassociated data base from which to draw inferences, Guardians. This conclusion set was only recently arrived at." A pause, and then the voice said, "We're working on this day and night, too, you know."

"Cry me a river," McKay said. "Guardians, out."

"This is ridiculous," Corbin said. He sat huddled around himself, shivering inside his coat. This V-450 lacked climate controls as sophisticated as those in the one that had been prepared for them at Heartland, but then that one had originally been built for the Guardians anyway, only winding up in the hands of its intended owners through a bizarre convulsion of circumstance.

It wasn't really that cold, although the storm wind blowing along the Missouri River in northeastern Montana beat like breakers against the hull. But Corbin was as tightly wired and nervous as a Thoroughbred. Pirelli, who seemed to be the high-strung one on the team, was not reacting at all to the aimlessness of the last three weeks. Corbin could wait motionless in cover for hours, even days—if he had a target. Without one, he found it hard to focus.

"They'll never find the bloody plant," the renegade SAS man said. "It's like hunting a needle in a haystack."

"Actually, it's rather more like hunting for a needle in a stack of needles," Peter Lynch said. "Even in a region as sparsely populated as this was, there is an abundance of factories in non-urban settings. Besides, now their search parameters have been refined, as that ghastly woman said."

Luttwak laughed. "To the state of Montana. An area larger than both Germanies together."

"Give them boys time," Cowboy said. He took a sip of salvaged Dr. Pepper bought from a store in North Dakota with good silver. The Liberators were dealing circumspectly with the people they encountered, asking few questions and paying for what they took, keeping a low profile—for now. "They're gonna find this here place, don't you worry none."

"How incredibly reassuring," Corbin said.

With a scream of fury, the wind launched a new assault fierce enough to rock the car slightly on its suspension. Millions of furiously driven snowflakes struck the vehicle hard enough that their impacts were audible as a sort of static through the hull.

"They have a lot of ground to cover," Luttwak said dubiously.

"Yes," Peter said. "But they also have the habit of success."

Luttwak laughed. "That's rather too metaphysical for me, my friend."

"If they don't turn up something promising in the next few days," Van Thyssel said, "I shall have to ask Koblenz for instructions."

"Their own bosses won't give them that long," Luttwak said.

"Our technicians haven't found anything in the Blueprint files about this mystery plant yet?" Peter asked.

"Nothing," Van Thyssel said.

"I say it's a waste of time," Corbin said. "They'll never find this factory. We should ask for permission to terminate them immediately and leave off this swanning about."

"And *I* say they'll find it," Peter Lynch said. "After all, they're almost as good as we are."

"Fucking Montana," McKay said. "Wouldn't you know it? It's always the last place you look."

"The Dead Zone," Casey Wilson said out of the blue as fitted a former pilot and practicing space cadet.

"We'll be crossing it soon, north of Great Falls," Sam said. "Then we can swing down to check out the neighborhood around Bozeman and Butte, and enrich Dr. Connoly's life by reporting we've made a circuit of the whole search area without turning up hide nor hair of our objective.''

Mobile One was sitting behind a long-deserted gas station on U.S. 2 northwest of Glasgow, Montana, being buffeted by the same storm as the Liberators' vehicle. Its heater was working fine.

''That's not what I mean, Sam. I mean, why not try checking out the Dead Zone?''

Sam looked to McKay, who was sitting cross-legged on an air mattress, taking his M-60 apart to clean it. It didn't need cleaning, as it hadn't been fired for days, but it was something to do. Tom had watch, which nobody envied him.

McKay shrugged. Every unit, no matter how small, has a flake. Casey was the Guardians'.

Dead Zones were the areas downwind of major concentrations of groundbursts. The pre-War popular imagination had exaggerated the fallout effects of even a major thermonuclear exchange to a sometimes ludicrous extent, envisioning strontium swamps and hordes of mutant monsters. In fact, most missiles fired by both sides exploded high in the air, producing optimum destruction but little fallout to speak of. Only against targets hardened to resist airbursts did the combatants resort to slamming warheads into the actual planet.

Hardened targets generally translated into missile silos. One of the biggest concentrations of silos in the country had formed an hourglass shape slanting across north-central Montana, roughly centered on Malmstrom Air Force Base at Great Falls. It had been a very popular spot with the Soviet Rocket Forces boys in charge of picking targets. The resulting roostertail of intensely radioactive fallout had swept down toward the southeast corner of the state, brushing the site of Custer's bad judgment call, and was just beginning to thin out when it reached the craters where South Dakota's Ellsworth AFB missile farm had been.

"Why should we bother checking it out?" Sam asked. "What are we going to find in a place where it got up to a thousand rads an hour for a while there?"

"It's died back to background everywhere but right around the craters," Casey said. He had the driver's seat swiveled around and was leaning forward, looking painfully earnest. "We've driven through lots of old roostertails. We've even found settlers in some of them."

McKay looked at the bolt assembly of his MG and set it down on a piece of oilcloth. "I get the feeling I'm not going to like what you're about to say," he said, "but go ahead and say it anyway."

Casey frowned briefly, not getting his drift. "Think of it this way: The area we're searching is, like, probably the highest-risk zone in the whole U.S. I mean, considering a space this big, why put a Blueprint facility here at all?"

"Principles of dispersion," Sam said. "There were a lot of Blueprint facilities dotted around the landscape. They wanted to spread them out." He grinned. "Anyway, this isn't quite the highest-risk region, not if you're just talking about fallout. The spot where the most potential fallout fans from likely groundburst targets overlapped was Heartland in Iowa, almost to the centimeter."

"Well, okay. But think about this: Why not put the kinds of facilities which are the least vulnerable to the effects of thermonuclear explosions in the highest-risk zones?"

"Yeah," McKay said. "And machinery suffers a lot less damage than people do from that stuff. Particularly heavier machinery. Radioactivity don't hurt it, and if it's sturdy, heat and blast don't affect it much unless they're pretty nearby. You get to something like a steel mill, it pretty much has to be in the radius of total destruction to be a write off. Makes sense."

"That's pretty chilling," Sam said. "To think of the Blueprint planners deliberately siting facilities in places they knew the personnel weren't likely to survive."

"Yeah, but the population of Billings, Montana, wasn't likely to survive, either," McKay said, "and as a matter of fact, they mostly didn't. *Everybody* was on the firing line for World War III. At least, Blueprint people knew the risks and volunteered to take 'em."

"So maybe we should search the Dead Zone, too," Casey said.

"Aw, shit," McKay said. He turned and stretched out on the mattress, leaving the machine gun parts spread out beside him.

Casey looked thunderstruck. "But I thought you said it made sense!"

"It does," McKay said. "That's why I said 'shit'. Skirting the Dead Zone cut our search area in half. We didn't have to mess with a chunk of Wyoming, half of South Dakota and Montana, and damned near all North Dakota. If our search area hadn't been cut down to just Montana, our dicks would really be in the dirt. As it is, we've got twice as much ground left to cover."

"Shit," Sam Sloan said.

"Well, we're here now," Casey said profoundly. "We can start out by checking this Dead Zone."

"Yeah," Mickey said. "Great." He sat up and glumly began fitting machine gun parts back together.

Central Montana used to be part of what the junior high school geography texts liked to refer to as the Breadbasket of America. Locals preferred to call it the Midland Empire, with excusable pride. Though subject to a fairly extreme climate, the Montana plains were fertile and well irrigated and produced plenty of good things like wheat, barley, and sugar beets. The less arable regions provided excellent range land for cattle and sheep. All told, the Midland Empire turned out enough food to feed millions.

Then they went and dropped a lot of hydrogen bombs upwind of most of it.

The Guardians headed south the next morning. They swung just far enough west to miss the tag end of Fort Peck Lake and headed into the Dead Zone, mostly following badly maintained farm roads. With its high ground clearance and massive suspension, the Super Commando had no trouble negotiating them. But the Guardians' kidneys and spines didn't thank them for choosing this route.

They were operating on a principle of favorable assumptions. They reasoned the Blueprint planners would not have placed the plant in the dumbbell-shaped area centered on Malmstrom, which had received the actual bombardment. Pinpoint accuracy for ICBMs was a myth, and anyway, the Soviets would be sure to saturate that zone with groundbursts so as to take out as many launch silos as possible. A near miss or plain overkill would wipe out the Blueprint facility just as thoroughly as if the Soviets targeted a warhead on its roof.

Of course, the Blueprint designers may have felt that was an acceptable risk. Maybe a two-megaton SS-17 had landed in the parking lot. Or the plant may have been in a Dead Zone in the Dakotas or Wyoming, or maybe they'd just missed it. The Guardians had no way to tell. So they just started with the assumptions most favorable to them and drove on.

Snow was falling as they drove into the Dead Zone, roughly following the course of the Musselshell River.

As they drove along a blufftop overlooking the river, McKay gestured at the viewports with the all-but-inevitable unlit stub of cigar. "I don't know why you expect to find any missing factories out here. Place sure lives up to its name—the Dead Zone. We've driven miles and still ain't seen nothing moving."

"It's *winter*, Billy," Casey said a bit plaintively from the turret. "You wouldn't see anything moving for miles if there never were a One-Day War, man."

"Ha," McKay said. He stuck his stub in his mouth and leaned back in his seat with his arms across his chest.

So about five klicks later on the road, such as it was, diverged from the Musselshell, they found themselves on a rolling stretch of plain, and they came over the top of a particularly high roller.

"So what are all them black dots scattered all everywhere?" McKay asked, leaning forward to squint through the forward port. Sloan turned the full force of a genuine down-home shit-eating grin on him. "Watch," he said, then hit the accelerator.

Lurching like a seaman coming out of his first bar after a five-week cruise, Mobile One took off down the slope. As the car came jouncing to within two hundred meters of the first snow-dusted black lumps, they suddenly jumped up onto four feet and went running desperately away from the vehicle with their tails held over their backs.

"Cows!" McKay exclaimed. "Well, fuck me blind."

"No signs of life for miles," muttered Casey, who was usually not such a poor winner. This whole Dead Zone approach was his idea, and he felt as if the others —meaning McKay—had put him on the spot.

"That's not all," Sloan said and chortled. "Take a look to starboard, McKay. About twenty degrees off our bow."

Two figures were racing forward as if to head off Mobile One before it reached the fleeing cattle. They were taller than the cows, and it took McKay's eyes and brain almost a second to get them sorted out.

"Cowboys!" Jesus H. Ronald Reagan Christ, actual honest-to-God cowboys!"

"What were you expecting, man?" Casey said peevishly. "Waiters?"

Sloan braked Mobile One to a stop. "That's enough. It isn't good form to chase people's cattle. I shouldn't have riled them up to this extent, but I couldn't resist rubbing McKay's nose in his vast wasteland.''

With an economy of motion that McKay's tactical eye could well appreciate, the two cowboys got the whole herd up and headed in the right direction—away from the enormous well-armed AFV that had just appeared over the horizon. In a short time the landscape was as lifeless as you could ask a Dead Zone to be.

"Maybe we should follow them," McKay said.

Rogers had gotten up off the air mattress and padded forward to peer out past McKay's shoulder. He shook his head. "Huh-uh, Billy. If they think we're after their stock, they'll be more interested in fighting than talking."

"Yeah. I guess you're right."

It wasn't that McKay was afraid of what a bunch of raggedy-ass cowpokes could do to the armored car with the Winchesters and Matt Dillon six-guns he assumed they carried—though there were enough light antitank weapons floating around the continent for him not to be too complacent, and never mind if they never had them on old *Bonanza* reruns. But it didn't make it any easier to win the hearts and minds of people if they thought you were trying to rip off their livelihood.

Having found what they were looking for—signs of human habitation within the former Dead Zone—they sat and waited for half an hour, giving the cowhands time to get their herds well away, and with luck, realize they weren't being pursued. Then Sam fired the engine up again and they set off, veering slightly back toward the river to diverge from the vanished herd's track.

Two hours later they came around another hill and found themselves smack in the middle of a full-dress firefight.

CHAPTER
TEN

It was dusk, which fell hard and fast at this latitude and time of year. A pickup truck with a bed built up by battered wooden planks lay overturned beside the same barely discernible track the Guardians had been following in the opposite direction. Figures lay clumped tightly around it in the snow, some sending flashes of brightness stabbing into the murk, others not doing much of anything. The wind, which had masked the sound of gunfire from Mobile One's hull pickups, swept falling snow almost vertically and sent clouds of fallen snow billowing along the ground like fog.

Fire stabbed back at the truck from the snowy waste on three sides. The distinctive ripping sound of full-auto bursts vibrated through the V-450's hull. Several riderless horses stood stamping and tossing their heads, none of them close to the upset vehicle. Men on horseback were riding along the road and splitting off left and right as if to take the truck in a pincers. Off in the swirling distance, McKay could just make out the headlights of a truck or jeep crawling along the road.

Then details of the scene began to register. "In-dians!" he yelled, as adrenalin distilled from pure as-tonishment jolted through his veins. "Attacking the truck—fire 'em up, Casey!"

"Wait!" Sloan and Rogers hollered at the same time. It was almost time for a shift change, and Tom was standing up front waiting to spell Casey in the turret.

McKay turned to stare at them. He could hardly believe what he'd seen, but he knew that he had: two men rushing through the snow, hunched low over long arms, long braids flapping behind, their faces dark and unmistakably painted in bizarre patterns.

"What the fuck?" he began, outraged at being coun-termanded.

Casey cut loose with a double salvo from the guns. Heads had already begun to turn toward Mobile One as the various participants realized spectators had arrived. Now an avalance of noise and fire got lots of everyone's attention. Way out in the midst of nowhere a line of grenade explosions erupted like a whole chain of min-iature volcanos busting loose at once.

"What are you—?" McKay tried again. His voice was weaker this time.

Soft-voiced, Rogers pointed out the obvious. "We best not start shooting people," he said, "until we know which side is which."

"Yes, but . . . well . . ."

He decided it had come to cost-containment time. His mouth was already as full of size-thirteen combat boot as it could get. He had been about to give a life-or-death command based on a childhood spent watching old Westerns on TV. He didn't even need the extensive training he'd been put through to realize with a snapped-elevator-cable feeling that this was not a good thing.

"Fuck," he said on general principles. "And we're not supposed to get involved in disputes between locals anyway."

"We're involved," Sloan said, leaning right to flick switches on the ESO console. "Time to start winning hearts and minds."

He patched the mike taped to his throat through the V-450's powerful PA system. "All right, people, we are the Guardians. We are official representatives of the government of the United States. We would be very much obliged if everyone would throw down their weapons and give us a hand sorting this thing out."

The cavalry had quite clearly arrived, equipped with enough firepower to grease Custer *and* Crazy Horse, Gall, and all their friends and relations without turning back for a second pass. Just who was being rescued from whom was no clearer to the locals than to the Guardians, but what was clear was that neither set of combatants was in any position to argue.

Everybody threw down his gun, got up, and began complaining at once.

"Oh, well, Jesus Christ," McKay said. He got up and opened the side hatch. He didn't bother to unlatch the Maremont; the indigenous forces showed a gratifying readiness to accept the superior moral force of Mobile One's big guns.

Tom climbed out beside him, his boots crunching on new-fallen snow. "Awright," McKay said, "just what the hell's going on here?"

It seemed both groups were more than willing to tell him the whole story. Simultaneously. In stereo.

"What are them riders doing, Case?" he subvocalized, waiting for things to settle down.

"They've stopped and seem to be watching."

"Smart boys. What about the truck?"

"Still coming slowly."

"He gets within six, seven hundred meters, give him a little reminder. We don't need anybody new joining the party."

"Roger, Billy."

A pair of spokesmen had pushed themselves forward.

There was a skinny white guy in a lumberman's coat, with frozen sweat caked in long, lank hair hanging over his forehead and clumps of snow in his beard, and a tall Plains Indian with a nose like the prow of a clipper ship turned upside down, wearing an Army jacket over a black turtleneck sweater, with a choker of long, narrow beads clasped around his neck. He had no facial paint, but there was a big feather stuck transversely through the base of his ponytail. They crowded each other to get into McKay's face, shoulder to shoulder as though they hadn't been blazing away at each other with automatic weapons not five minutes ago.

McKay got ready to bang their heads together.

"Gentlemen," Tom said, "one at a time, please."

His calm authority settled them right down. His gray eyes shifted to the white dude.

"Thank God, you've come," he panted. "These damned invaders would've overrun us in five more minutes—"

The gray eyes shifted right. The bearded guy shut off as if his switch had been thrown.

"These men raided our encampment before dawn this morning," the Indian said. "We've been tracking them all day."

"What were you gonna do if you caught them," McKay asked out of genuine curiosity, "torture 'em?"

Several Indians in the background made noises like they thought that was a mighty fine idea, but the spokesman frowned. "Take them into New Billings for trial, of course," he said.

"Kangaroo court," the bearded guy said.

One of his buddies muttered something about, "Fucking squatters."

McKay sighed. It was just too much to ask that anything about this snafu assignment would be easy. "Names," he said.

"Mike Rutherford, Montana People's Protective Association," said the beard.

"Jason Redfeather, Absaroka Nation. What you'd call Crow."

"I didn't know they could name Indians Jason," McKay said.

"*We* can name ourselves anything we want to, white eyes," Redfeather said with a grin.

"Right. So, this New Billings. It's the seat of government around here?"

"As close as we've got," Redfeather said.

"Don't listen to him, Mister," Rutherford said, pushing forward. "New Billings was set up by these damned invaders. It's not a legal government."

"Yeah," somebody shouted. "And who the fuck are you anyway?"

McKay stared down at Rutherford without approval. "We told you, we're the Guardians. I'm Billy McKay and this is Tom Rogers. More to the point, we're the boys with the heavy artillery."

"Hey, the Guardians, I know them," said another of Rutherford's haggard-looking followers. "They're some kind of Special Service troop, like the Green Berets. I read about 'em in *Parade*."

He had found the one and only way to get under Tom Rogers's skin. "Forces," Tom said. "Special *Forces*. Special Services is bands and barbers."

"Shut up, Kerry," Rutherford said. "We refuse to recognize the jurisdiction of the so-called authorities in New Billings. This is our land, and we mean to protect it."

He was practically standing on McKay's toes. "Back off, Jack," the ex-Marine growled, "before I bust some of your favorite parts."

Rutherford retreated hastily. "That's better. Now, is it true you raided these Crows' camp?"

"We never meant to hurt anybody. They're interlopers, and we mean to let them know they're not welcome to just walk in and take our land."

"They opened fire indiscriminately. An old man was

killed, several people hurt."

"Somebody panicked," Rutherford yelled. "All we were going to do was burn a couple of your trucks."

"Right," McKay said. "So what happens now is, we tend to the wounded. That your people's truck, Redfeather? Fine. Wave it on up. We are going to round everybody up and all ride off to New Billings together."

Rutherford's jaw dropped. "I told you, we don't recognize—"

"*I* recognize the authorities in New Billings," McKay said, "unless you or them show me something to convince me otherwise. You can take that as official U.S. policy, son."

A huge white man came flying between Rutherford and Redfeather, pummeling at McKay with fists like mauls. "*You fucker, you fucker, they killed Jody!*" he bellowed.

McKay took a step back, bringing up his right arm to ward the man off. Had he used his head, he could have given McKay a run for it—he was at least his height and weight and strong as a bear. But he was all over the place, crazy with grief and outrage.

McKay drew back his right fist, charged it with all 235 pounds, plus three weeks' stone frustration, and let it rip. It collided with the big man's bearded face like a freight train. The big man sailed backward with blood streaming from his face, bowled over three men who weren't quick enough to get out of the way, and landed spread-eagled in the snow, as if he were trying to make an angel.

"If you assholes still wanna play games," McKay said to Rutherford and his four men still on their feet, who were all gathered around their huge comrade, gazing down at him with very solemn expressions, "then climb back under that truck of yours. Then we'll stand off about a hundred meters in Mobile One and pop some forty mike-mike grenades in on you, and we'll just see who wins."

"We'll come," Rutherford said, "under protest."

"Smart man. All right, let's move 'em out."

To the Guardians' surprise, New Billings was not a town whose occupants had fled the encroaching cloud of radioactive dust or died in it. Driving in well after dark, the Crow pickup truck with the bound prisoners riding under guard in the bed, Mobile One following watchfully behind, the Guardians found themselves in a shanty town, a crazy collection of tents, burrows, trailers, and shacks cobbled together out of every sort of building material, salvaged or improvised. The glow of kerosene lanterns spilled out into the muddy main street from cracks in curtains. Otherwise, the town was dark and eerie.

"Many people who moved into the area after the radiation subsided didn't want to live in the old towns, even though they were largely intact," explained Redfeather, who was riding in Mobile One. "Not that there were that many towns hereabouts to begin with. But it's the same over toward the Judith Basin country, which was more thickly settled."

"Afraid of ghosts?" McKay asked.

Redfeather shrugged. "That or diseases."

"Is everybody here, uh, Absaroka?" Casey wanted to know.

"Hardly. There are perhaps two hundred of us from the reservation. If we prove we can thrive here, I think others will join us." He smiled. "We didn't exactly get the choicest land in the state, you know."

"I can dig it," Casey said.

Looking at him a little oddly, Redfeather went on, "I'd say there are eight hundred settlers around New Billings. Maybe a third are survivors of the old Billings, which explains why it's named that, even though the original's a good ninety miles away."

"Rutherford called you squatters," McKay said.

Redfeather's mouth tightened at the corners, and his

wiry panther body tensed. Then the tension surged out of him in a sigh. "He's right. We are. He belongs to a group which claims to represent a number of people who lived in the Dead Zone before, and have come back to reclaim their land. Or what they *say* is their land."

McKay glanced at Sloan, who'd shifted to the ESO seat after Casey took the wheel. The former Navy man kept craning his neck to keep in on the conversation.

"We have opened a can of worms here, Sloan," McKay subvocalized so Redfeather couldn't hear.

"You've got that right."

"Truck's stopped," Casey reported aloud. He pulled in behind it, and he, Sloan, and McKay stepped out with Redfeather to meet the mayor of New Billings.

New Billings City Center was a peculiar sight. A geodesic dome perhaps twenty-five meters across, with panels of some material fixed to a framework of joined metal pipe. The panels seemed to be all different colors, although McKay couldn't make out actual colors in the dark.

Inside, it was cold and dark and full of echoes. One of Redfeather's men started lighting kerosene lamps, and then it was a little less dark. Three other men herded the six prisoners in at rifle point.

"Far out," Casey said, peering all around the inside of the dome. The floor was plain cement, set with auditorium chairs arranged in a circle facing a round wooden platform in the center.

"Forgive the lack of amenities," said a man with a goatee and glasses who despite his small stature had to duck as he came through a passageway from the rear of the dome, pulling a Levi's jacket on over jeans and long underwear. "We're pretty rustic around here."

He stood up and adjusted his wire-rims on his nose as Redfeather emerged, bent over almost double. "We could light a fire," he said, gesturing toward a modern wood-burning stove set next to the podium.

"Thanks for the offer," Sloan said, "but you needn't take the trouble."

"I'm forgetting my manners," the small man said. "I'm Clark Maxwell. I'm what passes for the mayor of this town."

Standing as close to the dome's perimeter as they could without ducking, Rutherford and company scowled and muttered. Ignoring them, Sam performed introductions.

"The Guardians, eh?" Maxwell said, fiddling with his glasses some more. "I've heard of you. Seems to me there was some controversy about you last year or earlier this year—after the FSE invasion, I guess that was."

"It got cleared up," McKay said.

"As did the FSE problem, thank God. Not that they bothered us here. Now, what seems to be the matter?"

The story got told, with only a couple of disputes over details. The general outline agreed with what the Guardians had heard already. The raiders, who seemed to be unlucky as well as not altogether competent, had lost one truck getting away from the Crow camp, then developed engine trouble in the other, enabling the horsemen to catch up with them. Honors in the ensuing fight were fairly even, two of the raiders being killed —one, the driver, had been the brother of the big man McKay coldcocked—and one injured, while the pursuers lost a KIA and two men hurt.

Maxwell clucked his tongue and patted his hand on the cold stovetop. "Michael, Michael. You've really let emotion get the best of you this time."

"It's our land," Rutherford said, anger twisting in his face.

"Some of it is. But you won't be reasonable—"

McKay cleared his throat, heading off what he suspected would be a lengthy debate. "If we could, uh, your honor, we'd like to turn the prisoners over to you."

Maxwell's nose wrinkled. "We don't exactly have a jail, but I'm sure something could be arranged."

"What exactly do you plan to do with these men, sir?" Sloan asked politely.

Maxwell frowned. "Try them, of course."

"If you'll pardon my saying so, sir, that seems a little unfair. Your people and Mr. Rutherford's appear to be antagonistic toward one another—"

One of Rutherford's men laughed shrilly. The rest just looked sullen, except for Rutherford himself, who stood to one side with a thoughtful expression.

"What would you suggest, Commander?" Maxwell said irritably. "No courts have sat in session in these parts in quite some time."

Sloan looked troubled and started to flounder. "Well, it seems rather prejudicial, and we feel a responsibility for the welfare of these men—"

"You judge," Jason Redfeather said.

Everybody look at him.

"You're impartial," he continued. "At least as much as anybody is. As an interested party I'm willing to accept your judgment, though even as a war chief I speak only for myself."

One of his men looked rebellious under his paint, but the others nodded. Maxwell was scowling at the tall Indian. He seemed to feel Redfeather was trampling on his prerogatives.

"Bullshit," yelled the man who'd laughed. He had a thin face and pale blond hair, and looked to be in his early twenties. "You can't try us. You brought us here. You're prejudiced. You're the ones—"

"Close it up, Jerome," Rutherford said in a subdued voice. "They're the ones who saved our asses when we were surrounded. They'll be fair."

McKay looked at him, his eyes narrowed to the dangerous Clint Eastwood squint he used to practice as a kid. "You mean that?"

Rutherford nodded. "As a representative of the Montana People's Protective Association, I accept your arbitration."

"That's good, especially since we do happen to be official representatives of the United States government and all," McKay said, mostly for the benefit of Mayor Maxwell, who was still looking mutinous.

"Oh, very well," the mayor snapped.

"We'll check back with you in the morning, your Honor," McKay said.

"It's awfully late to find someplace to put you up," Maxwell said peevishly.

"Oh, that won't be necessary, sir," Sloan said.

McKay stared at him. "We'll be camping outside of town, sir," Sloan explained. "Meaning no offense, we don't wish to become too closely associated with your townspeople, if we want to be taken seriously as impartial judges."

"Have it your way."

"Are you crazy?" McKay hissed as they stepped out into the night. Snow and wind had ceased, and a few stars shone through rips in the clouds overhead. "We coulda slept in beds tonight. *Beds*."

"Well, yes, but what I told the mayor is true; we can't afford to be seen taking sides."

"And what is all this bullshit, anyway? We are under no circumstances to get ourselves embroiled in local affairs. Now you've got us playing Roy goddam Bean. *Jesus*."

"I didn't notice you taking up with the mayor when he wanted to call the whole thing off."

"That's different. He wanted to say we didn't have the right to do it. I wasn't going to let him get away with that shit, no way. But we're not supposed to get involved, and then you went and stuck us right in the middle of this mess."

"But we couldn't just turn those men over to vigilante justice."

"We are supposed to be making friends, so people'll want to help us find this frigging factory. You know what's gonna happen now? Everybody's going to get pissed off at us." McKay shook his head. "We're not supposed to get involved."

"Seems like we were already involved, Billy," Casey said. He opened the side hatch.

"Maggie's gonna have our asses," McKay predicted, then climbed inside.

"That's true," said Sloan. "All too true." He followed.

CHAPTER
ELEVEN

"Will you gentlemen have some more rhubarb pie?" Mrs. Corson asked. She was a cheerful pink middle-aged woman in a flower print dress, wool sweater and stockings, and white apron.

"I surely will, ma'am," said Cowboy, holding out his plate. "Much obliged."

Mrs. Corson beamed. "The missus loves to see a boy who knows how to eat," her husband said. He was a large man with a sunburned face that appeared to consist entirely of deep furrows, and a hard bluff of belly pushing out the front of his red flannel shirt.

The kitchen was crowded and dim, full of the heat radiating from the wood-burning stove and thick with humidity from the big cauldron of dishwater heating atop it. After the chilly steel confines of the V-450, it was paradise.

"So, tell us more about fighting the Effsees," the farmer said.

"Yeah!" said Terry, the twelve-year-old Corson boy. He was so excited by the exotic visitors to the house near Big Porcupine Creek he could barely keep his skinny rump on his chair. His freckled face glowed in the light of the kerosene lamp set in the midst of the table, from which his mother and older sister were busy cleaning the dishes. Beside him, his nine-year-old sister Sandy was fidgeting, too, but with boredom; *she* wasn't interested in a bunch of strange men with guns, and she wanted to get away and get back to the math homework the circuit teacher had given her. *That* was interesting.

The four Liberators eyed each other across the long kitchen table. "Well, you've heard about the uprising in Chicago?" Thijs van Thyssel asked solemnly. The boy bounced his head eagerly. "We were in on much of that—"

Corbin shook his head and stared down at the patched but immaculate linen tablecloth; he thought this whole scheme was daft. Peter Lynch just sat back in his straight-backed wooden chair with his legs crossed and a cup of coffee in hand, and Cowboy, seeming to engulf his end of the table, shoveled his third piece of pie into his enormous face.

Luttwak and Pirelli were in the car parked between house and barn, eating off plates Molly Corson—a haggard twenty-year-old widow who had received word of her husband's death in the counterattack near Leipzig thirty-seven hours before the One-Day War broke out— had brought them. The East German's heavy avuncularity tended to alarm civilians, and Pirelli couldn't restrain himself from getting into a screaming fight about the Historical Process or the Necessity for Armed Struggle with anyone he talked to for five consecutive minutes. Which hardly would have suited their cover as emissaries of the United States government on a vital top-secret mission.

Mr. Corson shook his head admiringly when Van Thyssel finished his matter-of-fact account of their part in Chicago's struggle against the FSE interlopers. It was actually a story from the Amsterdam rising in which the Liberators had, in fact, participated on the other side, but he adapted it skillfully, according to the dispatches he'd read from Chicago.

"I've got to admit you boys gave me quite a turn when you showed up this evening," Corson said. "Good thing Mrs. Corson was waiting supper for me to get back from the Protective Association meeting."

Mrs. Corson shook her head. "Those squatters. They'll be all over us like locusts if we don't do something. But still, I feel sorry for the poor things."

"It's our land, ma," Molly said in a dead voice. "We've got to be ready to fight for it."

Once the Liberators had confirmed the Guardians were headed for a cluster of dim lights that could only signify a town, they'd pulled back well to the east and decided to do a little intelligence gathering. They had heard the fight the Guardians had had with their superiors about heading into the Dead Zone, so it seemed clear they intended to pick a place as base of operations and scour the fallout zone, and the odds were good they'd light here. Now the Liberators were trying to get a line on how the terrain lay hereabouts. They were relying on their "top-secret" cover and the credulous patriotism of rural Americans to keep word of their presence from spreading.

"I thought you boys might even be Effsees yourselves for a moment," Corson said.

Peter allowed himself an ironic smile.

"Imagine that," said Cowboy with his mouth full. Corbin shot him a hateful look.

"We're a special unit," Peter explained. "When the War broke out, we were all at a special camp in Virginia, in training for an assignment of, shall we say, a very sensitive nature."

"Oh, wow!" the boy exclaimed. "CIA!"

"Shush, Terry," his mother reproved.

"The Cowboy and I, of course, are American citizens. But our comrades likewise volunteered to lend a hand to help America in her hour of need."

"It's a blessing we have friends like you," Mr. Corson told Corbin and Van Thyssel. "Terry, you run and wash your face, then help your mother and sis with the dishes."

"Yes, sir." He got up and came around the table. As he got to Corbin he stopped and looked curiously at the Australian's hands, which were both wrapped around his coffee cup. Corbin snatched them into his lap too late.

"Don't stare, son," his father said sharply.

"But, Dad, you should see this. It's neat. A dagger with wings, and it says, 'Who Dares Wins.' You know what that means? That's SAS!"

He stopped and stared at Corbin with his head cocked to one side. "But I thought SAS men never let on what they were."

Corbin brought his right hand up with a SIG-Sauer automatic pistol and shot the boy through the face.

His family stared in awful disbelief. Molly screamed. His face purple, Mr. Corson started to his feet. Cowboy grabbed the end of the heavy wooden table and drove it hard against the rancher's prominent stomach, pushing Corson back into the wall and knocking the breath from him. Peter Lynch pulled his P-7 from its holster and shot him twice through the chest.

Sandy raced for the door to the living room. Corbin fired twice more and knocked her sprawling. Mrs. Corson landed atop him like a plump harpy, squalling and clawing for his eyes. They fell onto the table and landed in a struggling mass on the floor.

Cowboy stood up, as Molly hauled open a drawer. It had been a long time since the folks hereabouts had been able to leave their doors unlocked at night, and with the road gypsies and all, they'd started taking precautions. Her hand came out with a little .22-caliber kit-gun revolver. She turned it toward Cowboy and shot him in his huge belly.

He grinned all over his face and came forward. She

emptied the pistol into his gut and chest, but the Kevlar vest he wore under his fatigues ate the tiny bullets. She grabbed the iron pot boiling on the stove, ignoring the way the flesh of her hands sizzled, and hurled the contents at Cowboy in a steaming cascade. He held his arms in front of his face and took it all. Then he came forward again, just grinning and steaming.

Like a striking rattler his right hand shot out and caught her by the throat beneath the chin. He lifted her up from the linoleum floor. She kicked him in the crotch, but he didn't flinch. He put his other hand on her head and twisted, snapping her neck as if breaking the vacuum seal on a jar of peanuts.

Corbin lay on his back, driving a slim Commando dagger into Mrs. Corson's body again and again. At last, she quit her shrill, furious screaming and went limp. He rolled her off him and stood up, bruised and covered with blood.

"Why the hell didn't you buggers help me?" he screamed.

"Wouldn't a been sporting, now, would it?" Cowboy asked. " 'Sides, you done all right with the kids, reckoned you could take care of an old lady." He was still holding Molly up against a wall with her slippered feet clear of the floor. Her chin lolled on his hand as he gave her breasts an experimental squeeze. "Nice titties," he commented. "Too bad I had to do her this way. She done shit herself, and here I'm so hard up even you're lookin' good to me, Corbin. But she done made me mad."

He let her fall and turned away. The skin of his forearms glowed angry red where the sleeves had slid down.

"You're a filthy great brute," Corbin hissed. "An animal."

Van Thyssel was still sitting in his chair. He had his face in his hands.

"It's your fault, you know, Neil," Peter said conversationally. He walked over to where Mr. Corson lay on his back, glaring up at him with insane rage and stirring his arms aimlessly as he tried to summon strength to rise up and avenge his family. Air wheezed wetly through the holes in his chest.

"It's that stupid ring you insist on wearing," Peter said. He shot Corson twice through the head. "It gave us away. Though I daresay we could have talked our way out of it, if you hadn't panicked like that."

"*I didn't panic,*" Corbin screamed.

He looked around with the eyes of a hunted animal. He'd had the ring made after his defection, as a symbol of defiance of the former comrades he had betrayed. He never took it off.

"Oh, my God," Van Thyssel kept saying in Dutch.

"You really don't have the stomach for this sort of thing," Peter told him. "You should have stayed a farmer."

"I'm a soldier. Not a murderer of children."

Corbin laughed. "You're a baby butcher just like the rest of us. You did your share in Europe. If we're damned, you're damned, too."

Peter tucked his pistol away. "Cowboy, you'd best get some ointment on those burns. And cheer up, Thijs, old chap. No one knows we're here. And I have a presentiment that in a few days the local inhabitants will have an explanation for this: another crime of the Guardians."

In the morning the Guardians rode out to parley with the Montana People's Protective Association. New Billings lay about seven klicks west of the Musselshell. By radio, the MPPA's president agreed to meet with them at a map reference about twenty kilometers east of the river.

The highway bridge on U.S. 12 a few kilometers to the south was intact. The Musselshell ran shallow this time of year, so Mobile One followed a well-used path to a ford at a place where the bluffs fell away, leaving flat land to either side, and splashed across. The sky was clear and very blue, but the sun shone without conviction.

The map reference proved to be a ranch house next to a line of trees planted for a windbreak. How much use they were with no leaves, McKay couldn't guess. There were several vehicles parked around the house when Casey pulled Mobile One to a stop. A pair of bored-looked horses were hitched to a post at the side of the house.

A couple of cowboy types in pinch-crown Stetsons and sheepskin jackets flanked the front door. They could have stepped out of a Marlboro commercial, except for the M-16s slung over their shoulders. They glared at McKay and Sloan from cold-reddened faces as the two Guardians stepped up on the porch.

McKay sneered back at them. *Whaddaya plannin' to do with them things?* he wanted to ask. *Nobody was killed yet with a slung rifle*. But they were supposed to be in diplomatic mode, so he kept his mouth clamped shut on his cigar.

The association's president proved to be a woman in jeans and a yellow cowboy shirt with mother-of-pearl snaps, short and wiry, with a face like an elbow and a rooster comb of stiff reddish-yellow hair.

"I'm Connie Witkowski," she said with a cigarette in her mouth, standing up to shake their hands. "So you're the Guardians. I've heard a lot about you. On KFSU."

Sloan and McKay stiffened. She laughed, a brittle burnished-copper sort of sound. "I never believe anything that little weasel says. Didn't before, and especially not since he started telling us the Effsees were our friends. Have a seat, gentlemen. Refreshments?"

She introduced the half-dozen males in the room. The Guardians sat on surprisingly dainty furniture, pale blue with little viney designs embroidered on it, and accepted cups of coffee. There was a fire going in the hearth, and

some inexpertly executed paintings of Western land-
scapes on the walls.

Witkowski sat by herself on a small sofa and tucked
her boots up under her. It would have been a kittenish
gesture if she hadn't been so homely and hard-bitten.

"You had Mike talk to me on the radio," she said in a
voice that was familiar with hard liquor and tobacco
smoke, "but I'm still not too clear as to why I should
buy your right to try us."

"*You're* not on trial, ma'am," Sam said, leaning forward and looking so down home and honest and
straightforward that McKay wanted to puke, "nor is
your association."

"Let me make something clear to you gentlemen,"
Witkowski said. "This is our land. We own it. We were
here before the missiles fell, and we— those of us who'd
survived the bombing and the fallout and the plagues
and pandemonium—returned as soon as we could to
take up where we left off. Doing what we've always
done: working the land for our livelihoods and the
welfare of those who eat our grain and beef and dress
themselves in wool from our sheep. We're natives.

"Then the squatters came. City folk, most of them.
Saying they had some kind of claim on this land into
which we'd poured our sweat and our very life's blood.
It is the aim of the association to drive those intruders
from our lands, Mr. Sloan. So maybe the association is
on trial after all."

"That's not at issue here, ma'am," Sam said with
dogged politeness. "The men to be tried allegedly committed acts of violence. That's what we're concerned
with, and it has to be looked into by someone impartial."

"What about the times they hit us?" one of Witkowski's companions growled.

"They're the ones we caught," McKay said. "If the
squatters try and pull anything while we're around,
we'll haul them in, too."

"Well, just what the hell gives you the right to come waltzing in here and start acting like judge and jury?" a lanky redheaded man demanded with a lot of Adam's apple action.

"We're from the United States government," McKay said. "We're under the direct command of the President himself. That makes us the only law west of the Pecos. Or are we east of the Pecos?"

"North," Witkowski said. She smiled. "I'm not any too certain of the Constitutional ground you're standing on, Lieutenant McKay. But as they say, extraordinary times demand extraordinary measures."

She leaned forward and stubbed her cigarette in a sun-purpled ashtray of cut glass resting on the low antique coffee table. "We've been needing some strong government around here for quite some time, Lieutenant. We consent to this trial of yours."

"We'll never compromise," Clark Maxwell said.

The Guardians had returned to New Billings to check on their prisoners and start setting out feelers—they had not forgotten their real reason for coming to Montana. The MPPA men had been housed in a cold cellar scooped out of the earth, which looked pretty secure and not too uncomfortable, being equipped with cots and salvaged candles. The prisoners seemed jaunty.

"They'd have hung us by now if it wasn't for you boys," a stocky youngster named Kerry had commented cheerily. "Reckon we could do a lot worse than have you sitting judgment on us."

Now McKay, Sloan, and Tom Rogers were sitting in the mayor's office, which doubled as the dining room of his modest house trailer parked behind the astounding City Center, as the town hall was called. With them and the looming Redfeather packed in together, it was a fairly tight fit.

The tall Indian frowned at Maxwell's flat pronouncement, but he said nothing. "Not that it matters," the mayor continued. "I don't know what that dried-up old baggage from the MPPA told you, but they won't even discuss the situation."

"They do seem to have a certain justification for their outlook," Sloan said. "After all, it is their land."

"Was." Maxwell leaned forward intently. "They ran off when the fallout came. When we got here there was nobody around. There was still some radiation; some people took sick from it. But we were willing to take the risks, Commander. For the land.

"We took the land back. Reclaimed it from the poison. Scraped away topsoil on acre after acre, to clear away the strontium and the other bone seekers. Burned off the tainted ground cover so that new could come up. Made the land live again.

"Then the owners started filtering back, acting high and mighty, thanking us kindly for what we'd done as if we were hired hands. Natives, they call themselves. And they call us squatters. But the land is ours now, gentlemen. We bought it with our labor and our lives. And the damned association waves pieces of paper in our faces and says it's got the law on its side. But they drive off stock and burn vehicles and shoot women and children, and I wonder just what the law from before the War would say about that?"

"That's what we aim to put a stop to, Mr. Mayor," Sam said.

"Perhaps there's room for both of us," Redfeather said, leaning back against the tiny butane stove. Maxwell shot him an angry look. "There's plenty of country here, and not that many of the original owners left. We could work something out. But they won't talk."

"From here it looks like they damned well better," McKay said. He stood. "Now, Mr. Mayor, we've got some questions we'd like to ask your townspeople."

"People in this town are busy, Lieutenant McKay. There aren't that many in town during daylight hours when there's work to be done. And at night they're tired." He stood up, too. "Now, if you gentlemen will excuse me."

They had climbed down the wooden steps butted against the trailer and started walking around the dome when Redfeather called to them.

"If you want to talk to people," he said, "you might try Bender's. Everybody goes there. It's on the road that leads east out of town and across Millsap Ford a ways north of the one you took this morning. You can't miss it."

"This a squatter place or a ground hog place?" McKay wanted to know.

"Both," Redfeather said, "and neither."

CHAPTER
TWELVE ───────────────

"A neon sign?" Billy McKay asked in tones of disbelief not unmixed with admiration.

"Far out," Casey exclaimed. "I wonder if it lights up?"

Bender's lay at the foot of a long mesa capped with rock, alongside a road that must have been graded at least once since the West was won. It was a low, variegated building, which seemed to have been patched together out of cinder block here and adobe there and generally whitewashed. The windows were covered with carved wooden shutters. A yellow sign with curlicues at either end and the word "Bender's" picked out in neon tubing sprouted at an angle from the corrugated tin roof, guyed by wires.

Leaving Casey and Tom in the car, ready for the proverbial quick getaway and keeping an eye out for trouble, McKay and Sloan deassed the vehicle, walked up and opened the screen door. A sign stuck on the hardwood door said OPEN—C'MON IN, so they did.

It was dark inside after the brightness of the broad

sky. They stood on the scuffed hardwood floor, blinking.

"Come on in and shut the door," a voice said. "You're heating up the outdoors."

"Oh, yeah." McKay shut the door. As his eyes adjusted to the gloom, he made out an old man in a black hat with a flat brim and a glossy black feather stuck in the band. He was wearing the most outlandish coat McKay had ever seen in his life.

"Afternoon," he said. "Are you Bender?"

"Oh, no," the oldster said. "I'm John Crow Hat. I'm an Indian. You might have seen pictures of people like me on old nickels or postage stamps, or maybe even in the movies."

McKay blinked. He looked at Sloan.

"And you are soldiers," John Crow Hat said. "You're welcome here as long as you don't break the furniture. Bender is very generous; he welcomes anybody. But he's very strict about that furniture. He makes it himself in his shop out back."

Sloan walked to the corner table, past tables and chairs that looked as if they could stand a fair amount of abuse. They were handsomely but not ornately carved. "We're the Guardians, sir. I'm Samuel Sloan and this is our commander, Billy McKay."

"I'm pleased to meet you gentlemen." He extended a hand but did not stand up.

Up close, he was a birdlike old party—bony and knobby with a big beak of nose and a mouth like two slits meeting at a very shallow angle. His face was dark and seamed like old and well-worn leather.

"Are you, uh, a Crow, Mr. Crow Hat?" McKay asked, belatedly joining Sloan. "You with Redfeather's people?"

"I am a Sparrow Hawk, yes, Mr. McKay. I am with myself, as you can see. Jason is a good boy, but his path isn't mine."

"That's quite the coat you have there, sir," Sloan said.

"Yes, it is, isn't it?" It was old ivory in color, striped horizontally with broad bands of red and yellow and blue at apparently random intervals. It made him resemble a large coral snake. "It is a Hudson's Bay blanket coat. It was made by a white man who was an enthusiast for the mountain men, who tried to live out on the Musselshell the way the mountain men did. That was before the War. But he found he didn't like it, and would rather read about that life in his books than live it himself. So he gave the coat to me." He smiled. His teeth were perfect. "Many strange things happen in this world. Have you got any tobacco?"

Apologetically, the Guardians were just saying they did not when they heard heavy boots thump the floorboards behind them. They turned around to see a large black man in gray mechanic's overalls and a dark stocking cap standing by the end of the bar.

"Thought I heard somebody drive up. Afternoon. I'm Bender."

Sloan performed introductions again.

"Cassie?" Bender shouted toward the back of the building. "Cassandra? We've got guests." He turned back to the Guardians. " 'Scuse me a moment. I've got to get cleaned up. Be right back."

Sloan and McKay sat down at a table next to the old man's. "We're lookin' for information," McKay told him.

Crow Hat nodded judiciously. "This is the place to find it. Everyone comes to Bender's."

"What may I get for you gentlemen?" a feminine voice asked.

They looked up. A girl of eighteen or nineteen, tall and slim and full-breasted with a great cloud of kinky hay-blond hair floating in a cloud about her shoulders, stood behind the bar.

"Your name'd do fine for a start," McKay said.

Her green eyes dipped briefly, shyly. "Cassandra, sir. Cassandra Morgan."

"That's a lovely name," Sloan said.

McKay shot him his I-saw-her-first look.

"What would you like?" she asked again.

"Coors."

"A Heineken, if you have it," Sloan said tentatively.

"We have both, sir. But they're not very fresh. And they're, um, they're expensive."

"We're on an expense account," Sloan said.

Crow Hat ordered his usual. Cassandra busied herself, then came out with a tray with three bottles on it.

"Thank you kindly," Sam said, accepting his beer and paying the girl in pre-1965 silver dimes—America's post-holocaust currency of choice, in spite of Maggie Connoly's efforts to get the country back on paper money.

McKay was staring at the dumpy green bottle that remained. "Perrier?" he said in disbelief.

Crow Hat accepted it with a smile. "Yes. The older you get, the more careful you have to be about your vices. This is about the only one I have left, except for talking too much." He said it wistfully, eyeing the way Cassandra's rump moved inside her faded gray cord jeans as she walked back to the bar.

"Come back and talk to us when you get the chance," McKay called after her.

"I have chores to do now, sir. But I will later, if we don't get busy."

Bender reappeared. He had on jeans and a green and yellow football jersey, number 67. He received permission to sit at the Guardians' table with his beer.

"Sorry for my rudeness. I was working in the shop when you came." He gestured around the room. "Got to get the place in decent shape."

"Looks pretty good now," McKay said, taking a grateful sip of beer.

"Thanks."

"So, are you squatter or ground hog?"

"I'm both. Ran a tavern in Billings—nice place, neighborhood bar, good steady clientele. Had a friend, a regular, owned a ranch out here, ran into money trouble back before the War. Lent him some, and he deeded me a few acres out here when he got past it." He shook his head. "He didn't make it out when the War started."

"Fallout?" McKay asked.

"Nope. He fixed his house up good, made it airtight so nothing could get in. Then he got appendicitis and died." Bender sipped his beer. "So, anyway, when the rads settled down, I went into Billings with a truck, salvaged what I could from my bar—few fittings, some stock, my sign outside. You like the sign?"

"It's, uh, unique," McKay said.

"I light it up for a while at night off an alky generator. Sometimes I have to pedal the old bike when the alky burner's down. So anyway, I brought it and some salvaged building material out here and built this place up. And as you can see, I got claims to be both a squatter and a ground hog."

He cocked his head to one side. "So what brings you out to this particular end of the earth?"

They told him.

"Well," he said, "you're welcome to talk to people here any time you like. This is neutral territory; folks leave their disputes outside. Settlers come in to drink, the natives drink and trade some—I run supplies of various sorts. Natives don't have a settlement like New Billings. You stay here long enough, you'll learn what there is to know."

He set his empty bottle down with a thunk on the wooden tabletop. "Seems to me I've already heard a bit about you gentlemen. Blew into town last night, caused a little bit of commotion."

So they told him *that* story, and how they'd found

themselves stuck as arbitrators of a range war.

"What makes it worse is that, as far as I can see, both sides are right," Sam Sloan said. "And they're decent folk. Some hotheads among them, but basically they're good people doing what they think's right."

"This bothers you?" Bender asked.

"We like to be able to pick out the bad guys," McKay said. Sam just looked chagrined.

"Not always so easy."

"What gets me is both sides keep talkin' about how they want the government back," McKay said. "What they really want is for government to come beat up the opposition for 'em."

Sam frowned. "You're being cynical, McKay. Surely they're entitled to a longing for order and the benefits government provides."

Bender snorted. "Like a chance to be part of a world war. Make history, like."

"People like to forget that what government can do for you, it can also do to you," Crow Hat observed. "Indians been learning that for a hundred fifty years or so."

Bender pushed his chair back. "Well, been nice talking to you, but like they say, rust never sleeps. You know, you were saying you wanted to keep your distance from both sides of this thing. You can put up here if you like. I've got some guest rooms."

McKay and Sloan looked at each other. "Beats hell out of that damned car," McKay said. "We'd be grateful."

Bender nodded and started off.

"By the way," McKay said, trying to sound nonchalant, "who's the girl?"

He jerked his head at Cassandra, who had disassembled a hand-pump dispenser and was standing behind the bar repairing it and humming to herself.

"Cassie? Just a refugee, lost her folks, wandered up with the first immigrants. Good kid. Knows how to do all kinds of things, real little mechanical whiz."

He went off to his chores.

"Easy man to talk to," Sloan commented.

"A good man," John Crow Hat said.

McKay was watching Cassandra with keen interest. "Gonna be a real pleasure stayin' here."

He felt Sloan's eyes on him. "After bustin' our buns sleepin' on that damned steel deck, I mean."

They made Bender's place their headquarters. After the frustration and strain of the last three weeks, to say nothing of the turmoil they'd left behind them in California and the horror that had awaited them in Colorado, it seemed like paradise.

As they'd been told, Bender's was the social center for a wide area of the winter-desolated plains. Daytimes there was a constant stream of visitors, customers, and traders eager to transact some business and tip a few salvaged beers or sample one of Bender's ferocious home brews, or just get a brief respite from winter, work, and loneliness. But at night the place exploded into full rambunctious life.

Drawn by the blinking of Bender's astonishing sign, dozens of settlers and natives would gather to drink and talk and dance, regardless of who they were and where they came from. Differences and weapons alike were checked at the door. People who tried to bring rivalries into the tavern were dealt with summarily, sometimes by Bender himself, wielding a baseball bat, but not unusually by the offender's own friends and neighbors. Bender kept a sawed-off shotgun under the bar, but had never had to use it, even as a threat. The prospect of being eighty-sixed from the heart of Dead Zone social life was the most effective threat of all.

McKay thrived in the honky-tonk atmosphere; it was his natural environment, even though the lights were kerosene lamps and the jukebox weighed heavily in favor of country. But all the Guardians enjoyed a respite from their military monkdom, stuck in the rolling iron hermitage of Mobile One. Casey danced with the best of them, with more fervor than skill, and Sam held court in the corner with his Missouri wit, taking more pleasure in the shitkicker ambiance than he'd care to admit. Even Tom Rogers relaxed the tiniest amount. And when the day's fuel-alcohol ration was burned up, occasionally one of them even took a turn on the bicycle generators that powered the jukebox and that sign. Hearts and minds.

Not that they forgot about their mission. They wouldn't have, even if Washington, which had been informed only that they'd settled into a temporary base of operations to gather intelligence, had had any intention of allowing them to. They were getting themselves accepted by the locals. They could have been resented as interlopers, but because of their policy of strict neutrality—and because they knew how to get down and party, in the service of the cause, of course—the inhabitants of the chunk of Dead Zone around New Billings warmed right up to them.

None of them warmed more rapidly than Cassandra Morgan did to Billy McKay.

"Some guys have all the luck," Sam Sloan remarked to Casey Wilson on the morning of their third day at Bender's.

He nodded from his cup of cocoa to a corner, where McKay sat at a table by himself telling war stories to Cassandra. She had on a standard working outfit, jeans and a sweater today, but she wore just a shade too much peach makeup and rouge, as pretty country girls do under special circumstances. Sam recognized the signs from his own youth in southeastern Missouri.

"I think she's mellowing him out," Casey said.

Sam looked skeptical.

The door opened and Tom Rogers walked in and sat down with the cold beating off him. With Mobile One parked out of sight in a corrugated-tin garage, and a friendly if sparsely populated countryside surrounding them, the Guardians had eased off from a field footing. But they hadn't entirely relaxed their vigilance. The former Green Beret had been checking out the vehicle and taking a turn around the premises, just keeping an eye on things. Cassandra reluctantly tore herself away from McKay and brought him coffee.

"Anything?" Sam asked.

"Washington called," Tom said.

"Complaining again, right?" Casey asked, moodily inhaling the fumes wisping off his Celestial Seasonings Red Zinger tea.

Tom nodded.

"I wonder if today's the day they'll get things straightened out in New Billings," Sloan said.

"Don't know, man," Casey said.

Tom shrugged.

Nobody seemed any too eager for the ground hog prisoners to get the benefit of their right to a speedy trial, including the prisoners. Both sides were making a big issue of gathering evidence and arranging for counsel for the accused and for the injured parties; neither the natives nor the Guardians would accept a settler as a prosecutor, so the case was as much civil as criminal. Fortunately, the incredibly comprehensive Guardians' training had included a sketchy course in rough-and-ready jurisprudence.

In spite of the Guardians' stated opposition, it was clear that both factions intended to try their whole dispute here, not just the accused raiders. Each clearly expected the awful majesty of the U.S. government, in the form of the Guardians, to intervene on their side once the facts were known. The Guardians were not any too eager for the trial to begin.

The door opened. John Crow Hat walked in, stringing a skinny kid of fourteen or so in pointy-toe boots and jeans and a wool-lined denim jacket along behind him. He walked over to the table where the three Guardians sat. McKay got up and lumbered over.

"My friends," the old man said, "this is Mario Anders."

The kid grinned shyly. He had dark curly hair, big brown eyes, slightly protuberant ears.

"I believe he knows where this factory you're looking for may be found."

CHAPTER
THIRTEEN —————————————

"Turn here," Mario said, pointing to a dirt track leading off to the left. The sun was bright, if not particularly warm, and ruts showed clearly through the threadbare coat of snow. The frost-buckled blacktop of U.S. 12 just a few klicks northwest of the ghost town of Vananda clattered like railroad ties beneath the cleated tires.

"You got it," Casey told him. The boy was sitting in the ESO seat, or at least in its general vicinity. He was bright-eyed and so full of excitement he couldn't hold still.

He was the son of an Italian-born mother and a father of Norwegian-immigrant stock who had been in the area since the last century. Prudently evacuating their ranch near the Little Dry Creek as the situation in the European land warfare that preceded the One-Day War deteriorated, his family had gotten out intact, and even taken along a few rams and ewes as foundation for a new herd. Like so many native families, they'd spent the months since the fallout faded struggling to make their land productive again.

Mario, it seemed, had an Uncle Lars.

"He was my dad's younger brother," Mario had explained back at Bender's. "He went off to college at Cal Tech to become a scientist. I was going to be a scientist, too. He said he'd help me get into Cal Tech, too, if I kept my grades up." He shook his head, his dark eyes solemn. "I did, too. But things didn't work out. I guess you know about that."

They'd nodded. They did.

Uncle Lars, it seems, had gone to work for the government. When he came to visit he claimed to be involved in a number of top-secret projects he couldn't talk about.

"Mom said he was just making that stuff up to make himself look important," Mario said. "She never liked him much. But I believed him."

About eighteen months before the War, Uncle Lars had turned up back in his home state, apparently for good. "He told Mom and Dad he'd quit the government and got a job with a big corporation that was opening a plant down near Vananda. But one night he told me a secret, made me swear never to tell anybody."

He paused, moistening his lips. "Go ahead, son," Rogers said.

"He said he was still working with the government. That some people high up were afraid a big war was coming, a nuclear war, and that they were secretly setting things up to rebuild America after it happened. He said that was what they were really doing in Vananda."

The Guardians looked at each other. What he'd given them was as fair a capsule description of the top-secret Blueprint for Renewal as they'd ever heard.

"So why are you tellin' us about it?" McKay said gruffly. He wanted to believe and was afraid to at one and the same time.

"He—he told me he might not make it through the War, if it came, and someone had to know the truth. He said that one day men might come looking for the factory. He didn't know who, but somebody from the government, looking for all the things that had been hidden away to put the country back together. And if he wasn't around, I was to tell them what I knew."

He took a deep, uneven breath. "And that's you, isn't it?"

Silence filled the tavern so full it seemed to press in on their eardrums. "Yes, son," Sam said at length, "that's us."

Uncle Lars's factory rested on high bluffs overlooking the Little Dry Creek, which was anything but dry. Patchily frozen, where it ran clear it frothed with runoff from the sun-melted snow. Maybe it used to be dry most of the time, but thermonuclear war had changed patterns of precipitation all over the world.

The dirt road wound through a crescent of low hills that bordered two sides of the plant. On the outside there was nothing to mark it as a Blueprint facility, which, of course, wasn't very surprising. It was big anyway. Counting the parking lot, a sea of cracked cement dotted here and there with a few parked-car islands, as if some industrious types had arrived early for a workday that would never start, the plant covered half a hectare of graded yellow earth. There were several huge hangarlike structures, and an assortment of smaller cinder block and prefab buildings that probably held administrative offices and the like. Around to the back a couple of semis stood, lonely and intact, as if waiting for Mad Max.

"I rode down here after we got back," Mario said in a subdued voice that barely survived the buffeting of the endless wind. "I was hoping Uncle Lars had come back. But the place was deserted then, just like it is now. Boy, my parents were sure pissed off."

He shook his head. "I've never seen Uncle Lars again, since that night he told me he was still with the government. He's dead now, I'm pretty sure.''

McKay pulled on a respirator mask with goggles, then waited impatiently while Sloan helped fit a borrowed mask to Mario's face and donned his own. Most of the really evil stuff had died down months ago, since high radioactivity translates into a short half-life. But in an enclosed space like this there would be potentially dangerous dust gathered in the crannies, and even crummy little alpha and beta emitters could fuck you up if they got in your eyes or your lungs. Low-level contamination like this didn't call for rad suits or anything, just covering up enough to keep dust out of your body crevices, a good brushing off when they were done, and some common sense. No biggie.

When the other two were ready McKay hefted a black Franchi fighting shotgun that bore a startling resemblance to a miniature version of the World War II German MG-34 in a gloved hand. A trophy of the Effsee war in California, it was an auto-loader with a pistol grip that permitted it to be fired effectively one-handed, and anyway it looked boss. ''Let's roll,'' he said.

Sam had his Galil/M-203 combo, with a multiple-projectile round up the pipe that made the grenade launcher into a giant one-shot shotgun itself. Mario had instructions to hit the dirt if anything nasty happened. Each Guardian carried a powerful flashlight in his left hand.

The nearest big building's door was locked.

''You gonna shoot the lock off?'' Mario wanted to know.

''Great way to collect a bullet in the nuts, kid,'' McKay said, ''and probably won't open the door.''

He reached back to his lightweight day pack. It carried a bunch of sophisticated stuff, including radiation detectors with alarms in case they ran into a pocket of bad gamma emitters. What he took out was a stout half-meter crowbar. He stuck it between steel door and frame and heaved. Metal screeched and tore, and the door flew open.

"Best lockpick ever invented," McKay remarked, sticking the bar back in his pack.

"What happens if they have a better lock?" Mario asked.

"You get a bigger bar."

Inside, the echoes of their footsteps chased each other around vast mounds of machinery and girders high overhead. There were big squat things that looked like presses, and clawlike manipulators that hung down from overhead or were mounted on carts equipped with six rubber wheels, and forklift-looking things that seemed to have no place for an operator to sit.

"Well, it looks impressive as hell," McKay said, craning around, playing his beam on gleaming metal. "Wonder what it does."

"Your Uncle Lars didn't give any hints as to what they made here?" Sloan asked.

"No, sir."

"Hey, look at this," McKay said, examining one of the front-end loaders. "There's a funny-lookin' camera on this sonofabitch."

Sloan and Mario joined him. Sure enough, a short pylon rose from the body of the loader, which mounted a camera with two lens tubes sticking out of it like a pair of glass crab eyes. Sloan flicked a coil of ribbon cable that led from camera to the vehicle itself.

"Stereo-optical computer input," he said. "It's a robot."

"I'll be damned," McKay said.

The manipulators proved to be mounted with similar video pickups, and while most of the larger equipment lacked such devices it also lacked the wheels and levers McKay associated with human operators.

"Whole damned place must be roboticized," McKay said.

"Made a lot of advances in that field before the War," Sloan said. "It was getting ready to be really big."

They searched along cement aisles, their boots stirring up dust their indicators said was mildly radioactive. That was what blousing was invented for, and Tom had stuffed Mario's jeans into his Tony Lamas and made them airtight with a turn or two of duct tape. They found robots of a startling range of shapes and sizes, but nothing to indicate what they were for.

Wind whistled among the hulking mechanical forms. Though the windows were mostly intact, the building wasn't terribly airtight. It probably wasn't intended to be. Once you got out of the primary blast-effects range of a thermonuclear explosion, a fairly open, light but sturdy sheet-metal construction like this, which let the shockwave just flow on through without offering much resistance, was damned near as effective as digging in and hardening, and a damned sight cheaper. No bombs had gone off near enough to produce any noticeable blast effects, but the place seemed to have been designed with them in mind. An encouraging sign.

Finally they reached the far end of the hundred-meter structure. Cleared floor space widened out to huge sliding doors. A front-end loader sat off to one side with metal panels stacked on its beetle-antenna prongs. They had a funny shape to them—a base and two perpendicular sides, then two shorter sides meeting at a shallow angle on top. They were pierced with meter-high oblong openings.

McKay scowled behind his mask. "Does this look like anything to you?"

"Uhh—"

"How about the end of a house? Just what the fuck is going on here anyway?"

They checked two more of the hangars. Then they busted doors in the cinder-block buildings till they found where records were kept.

Then they marched back to Mobile One.

Casey was leaning against the side of the car staring thoughtfully into the hills. "Ever get the feeling somebody's, like, watching us?"

"No," McKay said. He stomped.

Sloan was coming behind with his arm around Mario, who was crying his eyes out.

"What happened?" Casey asked in alarm.

"It's a fucking fully roboticized prefab housing plant," McKay said in disgust. "It's no more part of the Blueprint for Renewal than my bleeding piles."

"That's right, Washington, you heard me correctly. It was a false alarm. The kid's goddam uncle was hosing him, trying to make himself look big."

The radio in Mobile One emitted a strangled squawk. McKay blew up.

"Listen, Washington, we have run around looking for this phantom factory for the better part of a month with jack shit for clues, and all you can do is bitch us off. Well, fuck a bunch of *that*. From now on, we will get in touch when we have a solid lead, and *only* then —if we ever find out anything, that is.

"And in the meantime, don't call us, we'll by God call you."

"Shit," Neil Corbin said. "Shit, shit, shit, shit, *shit*."

Lying on his belly like a drab Gila monster, Cowboy lowered a pair of heavy binoculars, shrouded so the lenses wouldn't reflect betraying glints of sunlight to the unsuspecting quarry below. "Keep it down, there, boy. Like to take my head off with that caterwauling. Sound like a cat with its tail caught in a blender."

"One can sympathize," Peter Lynch said over the communicator in his prissy way. He was in the V-450 with the Aussie. "Our distinguished colleagues have just sunk another dry well, to use a regionally apt metaphor."

"Sumbitch," Cowboy agreed.

Van Thyssel stood behind the crest of the hill with his hands in the pockets of his parka and the hood down, staring up at a sun masked by a thin shoal of clouds. "Well, we must report it to Koblenz."

"They're pullin' out," Cowboy said.

"Then we should, too."

Two and a half hours later they were shadowing the Guardians back to their base, having followed them through a detour to drop off the dark-haired youth at an isolated house. They inferred from this that the boy was what was locally known as a "native" or "ground hog." They were avoiding contact with the locals, the more open approach having blown up in their faces. To get information on local conditions, they had fallen back on the expedient of catching a lone cowhand and leting Luttwak extract it from him. The last few days they had spent holing up as necessary in the broken hills above the tavern with the ridiculous sign, where they could keep the Guardians under surveillance.

To maintain secrecy, it had been necessary that two people who happened to stray into the wrong place at the wrong time be made to disappear, but they weren't unduly worried about searches. There was a lot of country to get lost in around here.

"I wish," Van Thyssel said, peering out a side block as he drove, "that we could see this land in spring. There would be wonderful wild flowers here, or so I should imagine." The short afternoon was already nearing its end. The broken snowfields were beginning to assume an evening gray.

"Bourgeois sentimentality," sneered Pirelli, who was riding a fold-down seat in back.

"Better be glad we got this nice snow on the ground,"

Cowboy said. His vast bulk was overflowing both sides of the ESO seat. "Keeps down the dust. Have a helluva time following these boys, otherwise."

The board beeped, announcing a satellite-relayed masercast all the way from Europe. Cowboy hit a sequence on the keyboard.

A familiar voice rolled from the speakers like molten amber. "Gentlemen," said Yevgeny Maximov in flawless English, "our technicians have been comparing the latest information you transmitted to the Blueprint files we have managed to decode. And we have for you momentous news."

CHAPTER
FOURTEEN

Down among the blinky-light panels in the communications center of the White House, the duty operator was roused from a half-doze by the harsh buzzing of an alarm. He blinked and twitched and spilled the open copy of *American Flagg!* comics off his lap, then blearily peered at a screen where a glowing code sequence informed him an ultra-high-priority call was coming through from the Guardians. Tight-beamed, and on the most secure satellite-relay channel.

He tapped a button that automatically broadcast a countersign sequence and asked for verification. The computer on the other end gave the correct answer in a billionth of a second, scrambling/unscrambling protocols were established, and the letters "OK" flashed on the screen.

"Guardians, this is Washington," he said. "Go ahead, over."

Even as he spoke he hit the button to call down the officer of the watch. After the blowup this afternoon, a call from the Guardians could only mean one thing. Especially coming in on this channel.

"Washington, this is the Guardians," came the familiar barely-muted bull bellow of Billy McKay. "Listen up and listen good. From here on in, we're gonna communicate only by the tightest-beam point-to-point laser-relay transmission. We're feeding you our coordinates now."

Numbers flashed across the screen. The operator didn't even glance at them; they were going straight into the best protected computer memory in North America.

"Any calls from any other map references you better track down quick, 'cause they won't be from us. And this is the only place you can reach us until we tell you we've moved. Got all that?"

The Tide Camp duty officer materialized.

The operator grinned up at him, gave him the thumbs-up. "Guardians, we copy five-by."

"Roger, Washington. We need a Blueprint recovery team on the ground ASAP at coordinates we're feeding now. We've hit paydirt."

Operator and officer cheered and slapped each other on the back. Connoly and her people had been making everybody's life hell.

"Washington, have you fucking gone to sleep?"

"Negative, Guardians. We never sleep around here. We have a plane and a team on twenty-four hour standby at Andrews. Pickup will take place twelve hours from now. That's 0423 your time. And we've got good news."

"What's that?"

"Your buddy Steve Tyler's riding shotgun. This is heap big medicine, and we're sending our big war chief."

"Great. Tell him to bring me some decent cigars. Can't get shit out here. McKay, out."

With a tiny click like a mouse flicking a cigarette lighter, the lock on McKay's door disengaged. *Here we fucking go again,* he thought, visions of Balin's Forge surging into his abruptly wide-awake brain.

He was off the bed and standing beside the door in a single noiseless leopard leap. Not behind it; a cagey bad guy might throw it open all of a sudden, right in his face. He was flattened to the wall on the other side, trusting that the intruder's attention would be directed to the bed. His .45 was in his hand, snatched in passing from its holster tucked between thin mattress and lumpy box spring.

The air was so cold it seemed to stick to his skin. The door opened halfway. McKay expected to see a gun barrel poke into the darkened bedroom. Instead a slim figure dressed in a long coat stepped quickly inside.

McKay hooked a burly left arm around its throat and yanked it up tight in front of him, pivoting from the doorway. He snagged the door with his right heel and kicked it shut. No point in giving any enemy reinforcements free entry. He jammed the Colt's muzzle against the side of a hooded head.

About this time he became aware of a faint sort of lilac scent, the glow of moonlight seeping in around the edge of thick curtains in long golden hair spilling from the hood, the firm-cushioned roundness pressed disconcertingly against the crotch of his skivvies.

Feeling sheepish, he relaxed his chokehold. Cassie Morgan stepped away from him, touching her throat with fingertips and swallowing. The hood slipped back off her head.

"How the hell did you get in here?"

"I got a spare key from Mr. Bender's office."

"You shouldn'ta come bargin' in on me like that. I might have blown you away."

"Please, don't be angry. I—I had to come." She went and stood facing the wall, as far away from him as she could get in the small room. She was barely visible in the darkness, a massless ghost form.

Shaking his head and muttering to himself, McKay walked back to the bed and sat down on it. He let in the hammer of the .45 and leaned across the bed to tuck it back into its holster on the side away from the door.

He wasn't exactly the retiring type, especially where women as attractive as Cassie were concerned—and most especially when they let themselves into his bedroom in the middle of the night. But he had things holding him back. For one thing, he didn't know whether Bender regarded the girl as his ward or even if he was getting it on with her himself for that matter. And Bender's continued good will was too useful to risk losing. There had been a time when Billy McKay tended to think with his dick, but that was before he became head of the Guardians.

Besides, there was something . . . something about the girl. Maybe innocence, maybe vulnerability. He couldn't pin it down. But, hell, he'd been talking with her three days and never once put the moves on her, in spite of the fact that she was a fox and obviously liked the looks of him, and it wasn't just because he didn't want to piss off Bender. Whatever had held him then restrained him now.

She sighed and turned from the wall. She walked toward the bed, smoothing her hair back from her forehead and shaking it out over her shoulders. It seemed to float, as if it had scarcely any weight at all.

She put her hands on his shoulders and pushed him onto his back on the thick mound of blankets and comforters. With quick, sure movements, she undid the buttons of her coat and shrugged it off. It whispered to the floor.

She was naked beneath it.

He could just make her out in the gloom, pale and lean and lovely, slightly bony in the hip and ribs. She knelt on the bed and threw a long leg across him and lay down on top of him. Her breasts flattened themselves against his chest. He reached up reflexively, felt goose pimples on the chill silky skin of her rump, felt her shiver against him from cold or passion or both.

Her mouth found his, and he decided he'd held out as long as duty demanded.

She was propped on her elbow with her shoulders exposed and one round breast cradled against his biceps. He lay on his back with the blankets pulled down to his sternum as she traced fanciful designs on his bare chest. It was colder than hell, but he figured if she could take it, he could, too.

"It wasn't my first time," she said.

"I sorta guessed that," he said. "Men got a way of tellin' these things."

She laughed and lay down with her cheek pressed to his shoulder. He reached across his chest and stroked her hair. It wasn't the sort of thing he usually did.

"It's been a long time," she said.

"I wouldn't think you'd have any trouble. You seem pretty popular around here."

She tore herself from him and sat up with her back to him. "It isn't that!" she said angrily.

He lay there for a moment staring at the fine contours of her back. Then, scarcely believing he was doing it, he sat up and touched her lightly on the shoulder.

"Hey, I'm sorry. I didn't mean to hurt your feelings."

Gradually the stiffness in her subsided, and she moved back against him.

They lay back down and pulled the covers up—like sensible people, McKay thought. She snuggled up and put her knee across him.

"There. That's better," she said. "I feel safe now."

She was switching back and forth so fast between mature woman, confident in her appetites and her attraction, and the shy kid she'd seemed when he first saw her in the bar, that he was bewildered. It wasn't an act. He'd seen the same unpredictable tendency to veer from maturity to childishness in a lot of people who were in their teens when the bombs fell. He just hadn't experienced it at quite this close range before.

He got an arm under her and held her against his side.

"Maybe that's why I chose you," she said. "It's not 'cause you're strong. There's a lot of strong men around here. But you're so—so certain somehow. There's like this force inside you, and it drives you on, doing what you think's the right thing, and never letting anything get in your way. And that makes me feel safe."

The conversation was making him feel uneasy, so he reached over and ran his fingers down from her shoulderblade, down her spine, and between the cheeks of her ass. He stroked a strong finger down the slit of her pussy, found her clitoris, and kneaded it gently. She shivered and seemed to melt against him. That was the best way he knew of distracting her.

She bit his neck. He growled and turned toward her.

"Guardians, this is Starship," Steve Tyler said. "Guardians, this is Starship. Acknowledge." He grinned as he spoke. He'd picked the code name himself. He'd always been a Star Trek fan at heart.

He was a long, spare man with a lengthy face, hair bleached white and roached up off his narrow forehead, a gold Mepps fishing lure hanging from one pierced ear, and a skeleton's grin. He rode up in the cockpit of the big Hercules, with the multiple panels of its windscreen opening the night right up before him. The open land's snow coating was almost luminous in the moonlight. Ahead and to the left a magenta sparkle shone like a jewel.

"Starship, this is the Guardians. We read you, over."

"We see your flares, McKay." There was no mistaking that voice. "We're going to circle once and come straight in."

"You got the goods?"

"Affirmative, McKay. Signed, sealed, and ready to deliver."

"The cigars or the other crap?"

Tyler laughed. "Have no fear, McKay. I've brought everything you asked for."

Riding aft in seats bolted down in the cavernous belly of the plane was the "other crap," a Tide Camp security team and a dozen technicians under the command of a Blueprint-participant engineer liberated from Heartland. It was pretty high-powered cargo, but evaluating a Blueprint facility for reclamation was no work for the second team. That was why Tyler was riding shotgun himself. Not to mention that it would be a kick in the ass to see his new old war buddies again.

The Herkie lumbered over the strip of Interstate 94 west of Miles City. The garnet glow resolved itself into lines of flares set to either side of the westbound lanes of the highway, pairs spaced thirty meters apart for a kilometer.

"Can we put her down on that?" Tyler asked the pilot.

The pilot nodded. "No problem. With these uprated engines and fancy props, we could land and take off again in that distance."

He tipped the Hercules onto the port wing. With the grace of a hippo ballerina in *Fantasia*, it pirouetted and came back over the Rosebud Creek, passing the line of flares again. Several klicks to the east he banked again and began a steep descent.

"Flash your lights, Starship," McKay's voice crackled in the headsets. "We wanna make sure you're on the right track."

Annoyed, the pilot glanced at Tyler. McKay seemed to be implying he didn't trust his flying skill. The Tide Camp chief shrugged. It seemed like an unnecessary breach of security, but . . .

"He's calling the shots," he said. "You got it, McKay."

Peter Lynch looked up grinning, the lights from the ESO board casting an eerie glow on his face, as the

C-130's huge landing spots glared into brief life like a string of supernovas and then winked out again. "I never turned in a finer performance for the Yale Rep," he said with becoming modesty.

"Well done, Peter," Van Thyssel's voice said in his ear. The commander was lying on his belly in the night and snow somewhere a couple of hundred meters ahead of the car and away from the highway, his Minimi machine gun set up and ready.

"Yeah," Cowboy said, hunkered down on the other side of the road with an RPG-7V antitank rocket launcher and several reloads. "Maybe you oughta retire an' be the new Rich Little."

Peter scowled. His flawless imitation of William Kosciusko McKay's voice and speaking patterns had been more appropriate to Rich Little than the Yale Repertory Theatre, as a matter of fact. Still, he consoled himself, it had worked.

"Luttwak?" Van Thyssel's voice sounded weary and worried as usual.

"Target acquired, Captain," the East German replied from the turret. The long slender barrel of the Rheinmetall 20-mm cannon pointed straight down the highway on which the car was parked. Straight down the center of the double row of flares.

"Corbin?"

"Ready, sir." The Australian's voice had a whine of irritation, as if to say, of course I'm ready, you tedious twit. Like Cowboy and the commander himself, he was placed forward to cover with his gigantic black Walther sniper's rifle, just in case.

Pirelli crouched behind the wheel of the blacked-out car like an animal about to strike. Fingers sheathed in expensive kid driving gloves drummed a constant rhythm on the wheel. Anticipation of destruction surged in his veins like an amphetamine.

The moon had long since vanished behind distant hills. The Hercules resolved itself out of darkness slowly, a gigantic bloated bat, engines droning. Reflections from the flares danced on its broad expanse of windscreen. Luttwak's finger tightened by micrometers on the electric firing switch as the tires neared pavement.

As the plane touched down with a squealing kiss of rubber on asphalt, the copilot craned his head forward. "The idiots are parked on the road," he said. "What's the matter with them?"

"You told them you could put her down in half that distance," said Tyler, leaning back in the navigator's seat. "They must trust you."

"I wouldn't—" the pilot began.

The humped form of the armored car exploded in frantically jittering flame.

Combat veteran that he was, Steve Tyler instantly registered the fact that the weapon inexplicably firing on them had a higher cyclic rate than anything Mobile One Mounted.

"Pull up!" he shouted as the right inboard engine blew up in a spray of sparks. *"That's not the Guardians!"*

The pilot was already hauling the Herkie's blunt snout skyward again. Even with one engine gone, the big plane leapt upward from the road with astonishing agility.

The vast viewscreen burst inward under a whiplash of 20-mm high-explosive sheels. Pilot, copilot, and Steve Tyler died instantly, torn to pieces in a stroboscopic hell of flame and noise.

"He's getting away!" Peter Lynch had shouted, pounding his open hand on the console. Sure enough, the aircraft was surging back up into the sky, its three engines whining into a higher key as one spectacularly flamed.

A line of yellow fire streaked toward it from Cowboy's launcher. The rocket burst against the fat steel flank as Van Thyssel and Corbin poured impotent fire into the plane. The shots had no more apparent effect than gnats biting a brontosaurus.

Then Luttwak found the cockpit with searching explosive fingers. The Liberators saw garish light flicker inside the greenhouse enclosure, and the Hercules waggled its wings once, coquettishly, before bellyflopping onto the highway.

Yellow flame blossomed, enveloping the fat fuselage as thousands of liters of aviation fuel exploded. The burning airplane hurtled along the road exactly as if it were on rails.

"Pirelli!" Peter shrieked. The Italian terrorist stared as if hypnotized at the gigantic fiery apparition bearing down on them. Peter clutched frantically for the wheel. Pirelli snapped out of it, gunned the engine to a hysterical growling wail, and spun the wheel.

The Super Commando plunged down the embankment. Like a blazing freight train, the airplane rushed past in a cataclysm of noise, roaring fire and explosions, and grinding, tortured screams of metal on pavement. It skidded on another half a kilometer, slowly rotating counterclockwise, and came to rest broadside to the highway.

Like men reprieved from execution, Peter and Pirelli stared at each other. Then they pounded each other on the back and cheered as Cowboy vibrated their skulls with an old-fashioned rebel yell.

The other Liberators hustled back to the vehicle, flushed with cold and victory. Pirelli headed north, leaving a giant pyre blazing behind them. They had another plane to catch in just a few hours.

CHAPTER
FIFTEEN

"So what's the news across the nation, Frank?" Bender asked, standing behind the bar polishing beer mugs.

The trader took a gulp of rum-laced coffee. He was an amazing-looking specimen. He was about Sam Sloan's height, a touch under six feet, lean as a slat in a long duster coat and cowboy boots. He had a face that seemed to consist mostly of long, narrow chin and nose, black mustache, and a black patch over one eye. He wore a black hat with a flat brim and a flat crown.

"Things're in a state of flux, Bender, a state of flux. Now that the Effsees are gone, a lot of local leader types are beginning to poke their heads up and look around."

Sam Sloan nodded sagely. "Local governments beginning to reassert control, establish order."

The trader cawed a laugh. "Seems more like the little sharks beginning to reassert their appetites, now the Great White's gone away."

He accepted an invitation nodded by McKay to take a place at the Guardians' customary corner table. Cassie came over and took his order for scrambled eggs and bacon for breakfast, gave McKay a warm smile, and turned away. The flush in her cheeks this morning wasn't rouge.

Sloan cocked an eyebrow at McKay. Instead of smirking, McKay poked his nose into his own mug.

"Chicago's been split up into five, six fiefs. Seems like every damn guerrilla leader from the uprising's taking personal credit for the Effsees pulling out, claiming sovereignty over what's left of the city. Detroit's new straw boss just cleaned out the last of his competition. Word is he's already invaded Windsor, over on the peninsula in Ontario, and they even say he's putting together a battle fleet. He says he's only interested in fostering peaceful trade on the Great Lakes, but since he calls himself the Motor City Madman, I don't know how much credit you can give to that."

He pulled a long and slender black cigarette from an inner pocket of his coat and lit it, completing his resemblance to a character in a spaghetti western.

"Everybody's favorite evangelist, old Forrie Smith, is putting together an army in Oklahoma. Hiring a lot of mercenaries, I'm told. You boys might be interested in looking into that sometime—oops, never mind, forgot who I'm talking to. Anyway, he's been making noise about reconquering America for Christ and the memory of Wild Bill Lowell, as you probably heard on his ever-popular radio broadcasts."

"We heard," McKay said.

He nodded. "Well, rumor says what he's really interested in is grabbing off parts of the old Dead Zones in Kansas and maybe Nebraska. Settlers've been moving back in, reclaiming farmland, just like around here. We could maybe see a real struggle shape up for the bread-basket regions here in the next few years. Could be he's interested in stealing a march on the competition."

"Bummer," Casey Wilson said.

"We're gonna have to squash that little son of a bitch one of these days," McKay commented.

"Best of luck," Frank said laconically.

"What do people say about President MacGregor and the government in Washington?" Sam asked.

The trader gave him a quizzical look. "Well, not a whole lot, to tell you the truth. Washington's a long way off. Some people think the government got them into this mess in the first place. Bunch of others don't know what to think, since that whole mess with Lowell and then the Effsees coming in." He took another gulp of his coffee. "Most people I talk to got more immediate concerns, when you get right down to it."

His breakfast arrived. He paid Cassie and squeezed a tip into her hand. She smiled politely, but her eyes kept straying to McKay.

"Cute little piece," he commented as soon as she swayed out of earshot. "Seems sweet on you, mister."

"We're just good friends," McKay said in a tone that didn't encourage further discussion.

The trader shrugged. "Well, anyway. They've gotten pretty uptight down Texas way, or so I hear, since the president of Mexico got shot last week—"

"He did?" Sam Sloan asked, startled.

"Yeah. The news was all over the radio, from KFSU to some French channel out of Quebec."

"We've been out of touch," McKay said.

As he ate, he filled them in on more of what had been going on since the Effsee pullout. He had stories from everywhere, from a fresh epidemic in Florida to a General Dean gathering military remnants in Oregon and claiming to be with the legitimate government of the United States. Most of it was hearsay, he admitted. But even after the electromagnetic pulses of the War, a good deal of electronic communications equipment still survived, so word got passed around quite quickly, if irregularly. It was part of his business to gather as much of such information as he could and evaluate it.

"Caught some interesting gossip on the drive in," he mentioned. "Some strange rumors floating around—

lights in the sky at night, armored cars driving around, a big fire down on the Rosebud last night or this morning. Saw a great big airplane way up in the sky myself, headed south, maybe two hours ago. Couldn't say what kind it was.''

"We've been driving around in an armored car,'' Sloan said. "The other sightings I couldn't explain.''

"Like, what brings you this way?'' Casey asked.

"Got a truck outside loaded with batteries, cassette tapes—some of 'em brand new, out of Nashville, if you're interested—medical supplies, and primers for reloading ammunition, rifle and pistol both. Truck runs on gas, alky, or methane. I've rigged her up and pulled her with mules more than once or twice. That's an item in demand these days, by the way. Mules. Stronger and smarter than horses, and you don't have to adjust their carburetors or refine or distill their fuel.''

He shrugged. "Mostly, I'm taking a swing out to the coast, to see what people want and need so I can go larger scale. That and doing a little bird watching.''

"Bird watching,'' McKay said.

"Yessir. Just in the last week, I've seen fine specimens of four species that used to be on the endangered list, and one that was supposed to be extinct.'' He shook his head. "Happens to me a lot. Bunch of curious things have happened since the War.''

"You can say that again,'' Sam Sloan said.

They went into New Billings before noon to discover that both sides of the upcoming trial had gotten all their preparations out of the way and were suddenly eager to get it all over with. The Guardians had some leads to follow up on, without having much faith they'd pan out, so the trial was set for tomorrow.

Since the leads failed to amount to anything quickly enough, the Guardians were back at Bender's when it started to get dark after four. They were depressed and discouraged. Washington wasn't on their case on an hourly basis any more, but their own sense of mission was beginning to prey on their minds. They were getting nowhere fast, and couldn't hide from the fact.

They'd just finished dinner when a call came in from Connie Witkowski of the MPPA. "Something's come up," she said, her voice even huskier than usual. "I need you to come out. Immediately."

"Can't you tell us what it's about?" Sam asked.

"I can't talk over the radio. Please—it's urgent."

She broke the connection. Huddled around Bender's radio in an office cluttered with tool catalogs and autographed photos of baseball stars, the Guardians looked at each other. Witkowski hadn't struck any of them as the sort to plead unless things were serious.

"Think she may have learned something about the factory?" Casey asked.

"I don't think so," Sam said. "She sounded worried to me."

"We ain't gonna know till we go find out," McKay said. "So let's drive on."

Cassie clung to him as they walked out to the shed where Mobile One was parked, hidden from view. Tonight was a regular customer's birthday, and in honor of the occasion she had on an unbearably cute little outfit consisting of a pink and yellow cowboy shirt with pearly snaps, a short denim skirt, and cowboy boots worn over nylons. She held a white cowboy hat in one hand and shivered.

"I hate to let you go," she said.

Embarrassed, he disentangled himself from her as gently as he could. "I've got to go away for good sometime, Cassie."

"I know. But I like to pretend that won't ever happen."

Suddenly tears filled her eyes, glittering with the mutable light of Bender's sign. "I—I feel like I may never see you again."

"Oh, bullshit, we're just riding a few klicks over to

Withowski's house," MacKay said.

But she had turned and raced back inside as if fleeing from him. He shook his head and clambered into the steel womb of Mobile One.

"Fire ahead, Billy," Casey Wilson said.

McKay came forward. An orange glow ahead suffused the horizon beyond some hills, reflecting off a bank of low clouds. It could have been the moon rising behind haze, but the moon was already up, and you didn't see that sort of petrochemical filtering effect much since the War.

"That's a house burning, Billy," Tom said from the turret.

"How can you tell that?" Sloan asked.

"Just can."

"He's right," McKay said. He and Tom Rogers had fought a different war from the fighter jock and cruiser officer before they upped with the Guardians. A dirtier, uglier, more personal war. They'd seen bonfires made from homes before. "Hard to mistake it for anything else once you get used to it. There's just something about it."

"It's right on our course," Sloan said. He didn't even have to check the digital compass display on Casey's board.

"Uh, yeah," McKay said. Something stirred down in his gut and ruffled the short hair at the back of his neck. "Cruise on. Not too fast, and stay ready to blast or boogie."

Several klicks rolled by with excruciating slowness. The glow got brighter, and they could make out the characteristic flicker of fire now. By the time they reached the last hill before the MPPA leader's house, nobody had any doubt of what they'd see when they reached the crest.

Still, it hit like a blow. The neat two-story house was bleeding flame into the sky from doors and windows like wounds. There was no sign of life anywhere around.

"That's strange," Sloan said. "Country people like this, I'd think they'd be crowding around to lend a hand."

With a whir of servos, the turret traversed. "Take a look to the north," Tom said.

The other three crowded around Casey's port-side viewport. There was another orange glow faint on the horizon.

Sam frowned. He had a headset on, monitoring radio traffic at random—AM, FM, shortwave, CB—you could never tell where you might pick up something useful or maybe vital. Talking with the trader today had made them conscious of what they'd missed by not paying enough attention to the radio. But what caught his attention was the computer, automatically overriding the channel he was listening in on because it had detected a signal relatively nearby.

"I've got something," he said.

"Put it on," McKay said.

"—come back," a woman's voice was saying hysterically. "I heard their engine again."

"Calm down, Laurie. Get the kids and pull out. Has anybody seen their car?" It was a male voice. Several others responded in the negative.

"But what can we do?" a voice yammered. It was so wrenched with panic the Guardians couldn't tell whether it was male or female. "We can't touch them!"

"Easy, now, easy," the first male voice said. "Just keep out of their way. It's all we *can* do."

"We never should have trusted those fucking Guardians," another voice said.

"Freehold," Sam Sloan said in a voice cracked like old ice. "It's Freehold all over again."

"Holy shit," McKay said. "Casey, get us back to New Billings in one hell of a hurry."

• • •

They saw the flames before they crossed the Mussel-shell. "I can't believe this is happening," Sam Sloan said. "It's like a nightmare."

"Drive on," McKay commanded harshly. Casey licked his lips and drove. His face was pale.

A mob met them at the outskirts of the crazy-quilt town, armed with rifles and axes and bricks—anything that came to hand. Behind them, flames capered like mad giants among the buildings.

"So you got the nerve to show yourself this time," somebody shouted, "not just shell us from the dark like cowards."

"Whatever happened here, we had nothing to do with it," McKay said, his voice amplified by the loud-speaker.

He squelched the PA. "Jesus, where have we heard *that* before?"

"You expect us to believe that?" somebody else yelled. "Who else has got guns like that?"

"Mayor Maxwell's dead," a woman screamed. "God knows how many other people are dead or injured. Did you come back to finish us off?"

"Listen, I'm telling you—"

A brick bounced off the viewport, right in front of his face. Shots cracked out of the crowd and clanged off the hull. Somebody threw a Molotov, and the street flooded with fire in front of the car.

"Jesus," McKay repeated. "Casey, get us the hell out of here, or we're gonna have to grease some of these people for true."

The car lurched backwards, heeling way over as Casey turned it 180 degrees. Rocks and bullets bounced off the armor as Mobile One sped away from the stricken town.

Casey bit his lip and looked as if he wanted to cry. He didn't have to ask where to go next.

The neon sign hung from broken guys. Most of its

glass had been punched out by the same bullet storm that had riddled the door and shattered the windows. A jeep and two pickups were parked on the packed dirt out front, likewise shot to shit.

Sam moaned.

"At least there was a fight here," Casey said, forcing optimism.

"This wasn't no fight," Tom said. "It's vandalism."

"He's right," McKay said, swallowing bile. "Somebody just fired the place up at random with a machine gun."

He picked up his black Franchi submachine gun. "Cover us," McKay said, then climbed out. Sloan followed with his Galil-203.

McKay paused at the door to finger splinter-rimmed holes in the solid door. "Five-five-six," he said.

He stepped to the side and pushed the door open, then pivoted quickly through and stepped aside to put the wall at his back. It was reflexive precaution; he knew damned well there were no bad guys inside. If he'd thought there might be, he would have led off with a stun grenade, and then he and Sloan would have gone in high right/low left.

"Shit," he said.

It looked as if a cyclone had hit. Tables and chairs lay overturned, mingled with unmoving bodies. The bottles behind the bar had been blasted to shards that glimmered in the light of an overturned kerosene lantern.

Sam stooped to turn over a slight body lying on its stomach. "Oh, no," he said, "no, no, no."

It was John Crow Hat. From the looks of the front of what had been a plaid flannel shirt, he'd absorbed a shotgun blast from close enough to grab the barrel. He was dead.

McKay stumbled toward the bar as if he had a cable noose around his neck and was being winched inexorably forward.

Cassie lay amidst shattered glass and spilled booze

and blood. Her legs, spread wide, hung over the end of
the bar, her feet still encased in ornately worked cowboy
boots with pointed toes. Her skirt was up around her
belly. Her panties had been torn or cut away. Her shirt
was ripped open. A long butcher knife had been driven
through her sternum with incredible force, pinning her
to the hardwood bar. There were cigarette burns on her
belly and breasts and thighs. Her face had set into an
eternal mask of horror, cornflower eyes staring, a
trickle of blood running from mouth to the little fake
pearl in one pierced earlobe and caking in her hair.

McKay turned and brought his left fist crashing down
onto the bar. Inch-thick oak cracked.

A foot crunched broken glass. Standing horrorstruck
amid the devastation, Sam whirled, bringing up his
weapon. McKay raised his shotgun one-handed, like an
oversized pistol.

Bender stood in the door to the back. His face seemed
to have been dusted with gray wood ash. The front of
his coveralls was soaked with blood. He held a sawed-
off shotgun in his hands.

For a moment, he and the Guardians faced each
other, their weapons aimed. Then the black man
croaked, "Oh, it's you."

The twin barrels of the shotgun swung right. One
went off, blasting a shower of whitewash flakes from
the wall. Then Bender's knees gave way, and he pitched
forward on his face.

CHAPTER
SIXTEEN

They laid the tavern keeper on the deck in Mobile One. Tom Rogers cut open his coveralls and the work shirt beneath while Sloan took over in the turret. Bender had taken two bullets in the chest and one in the left shoulder. Nine millimeter, by the size of the entrance wounds, though it was impossible to tell for sure.

Bender's eyes fluttered open as Rogers worked at debriding the wounds. He moaned. Rogers paused to hypospray anesthetic into his arm.

"We—thought we heard you drive up," Bender wheezed.

"Don't talk," Rogers said.

McKay glared at him. They needed information badly. But when Rogers was in medic mode, concern for his patient overrode almost everything else.

But Bender shook his head feebly. "Gotta . . . tell you."

"Good man," McKay said.

"F-four of them. Handsome dude, a heavyset guy with dark hair, a—a little rat-faced guy, and this great big fat peckerwood sorta dude. They just—came in—and started shooting.''

He coughed violently. Rogers leaned close, but no blood came up. "Really, Mr. Bender, you shouldn't try to talk.''

Bender waved him weakly away.

"Did they say anything?" McKay asked.

"Not at first. Heard 'em . . . talk, after I got hit. They're not . . . not all American. Little guy had a, a funny accent. Italian or French. B-balding guy, the stocky one . . . he talked like a German.''

"They spoke English?"

He nodded.

"Did they say why they were doing this?''

"Said—said they were driving the last nail in—the Guardians' coffin. Laughed a lot . . . about that. Then they, they started in on Cassie. I tried to get up—blacked out—'' He turned his head from side to side, tears pouring from his eyes. "Oh, Cassie, Cassie, I couldn't—couldn't protect you—''

McKay squeezed his eyes tight shut.

"Billy,'' Casey said. He was holding one earphone of the ESO headset to his ear. "I think you ought to hear this.''

McKay nodded wearily for him to put it on the internal speaker. A familiar voice filled the vehicle.

"—regret very much to announce,'' said President Jeffrey MacGregor, "that early this morning a United States Air Force plane, carrying technical personnel on a mission of utmost importance to the welfare of this nation, was ambushed and destroyed by the four men known as the Guardians. For what reasons, I cannot imagine—and have no wish to—they have turned renegade. Therefore, effective immediately, I disavow them and any actions they might undertake in my name, or that of the United States of America.''

"We're fucked,'' Billy McKay said. He sat on a fold-down seat and stared at his hands as if looking for bloodstains.

Rogers finished bandaging Bender. "Wounds look clean," he remarked as if nothing out of the ordinary had happened. "He's got a chance."

"Billy," Casey said, almost pleading, "what's *happening?*"

McKay just shook his head. He had no more energy left inside him. He had no more anything left inside him.

"Isn't it obvious?" Sloan asked, his voice hard and bright as glass. "It's the same men who hit Vista and Freehold. We've been set up again."

"Did a hell of a job on us this time," McKay said. "We're fucking Public Enemy Number One as of now."

"Why did they wait this long to hit us again?" Casey asked. "Why now?"

Rogers laid a blanket over Bender and tucked in the edges. "That's obvious, too," he said. "Think about what's happened in the last twenty-four hours."

"I can't think of fucking anything," McKay said.

"Think about being a Guardian."

Rogers's words came soft, but they rang like a death knell. For a moment longer, McKay stared downward, and then he raised his head and looked at the former Green Beret. His blue-white eyes blazed like headlights.

Casey tensed, afraid McKay would go for Rogers. Tom knelt imperturbable as Buddha.

"Yeah," McKay spoke at last in a voice broken like the glass on the bar where Cassie lay. "Yeah, you're right, Tom. You're always right. Maybe you ought to be head of this chickenshit outfit. I've been doing a piss-poor job lately."

He dropped his eyes again, and his head drooped as if it had suddenly gotten too heavy for even his bull neck to hold upright. "I've been flying off the handle, making bad judgment calls, just plain not thinking. Now

I'm sniveling like a draftee with one nut shot off. Maybe I ain't fit to command."

"You're our leader, Billy," Tom said.

"That goes for me, too, man," Casey said.

"And me, too, McKay," said Sloan.

A shudder passed through McKay like the San Andreas slipping a few more centimeters. When he raised his head his eyes were still incandescent, but they burned with a different fire.

"All right," he said. "If you swingin' dicks are still fool enough to follow, I guess I gotta lead. Now, what was that you said, Tom? Something about the last twenty-four hours?"

Abruptly, Sam laughed. "Jesus. Oh, Jesus. We've been had, McKay. We've been fucking had."

"We shall require at least twenty-four more hours to evaluate this facility, Captain Van Thyssel," Dr. Roulade said, his English heavily accented with French. He was a middle-sized man with a jumbo-sized head fringed with wiry-wild Albert Einstein hair. The fluorescent lights of the commissary in a low prefab structure next to the three huge hangarlike buildings gleamed on his bald cranium. "How much more time we shall require to decontaminate and disassemble the equipment and prepare it for shipment, I cannot even conjecture. Are you absolutely certain you can provide for our security, Captain?"

"My men are in place," interjected Captain Lavrentin, "equipped with the most modern night-vision equipment. We can handle any threat from the inhabitants of the area." A full captain was more rank than generally called on to command a squad of twelve Soviet paratroopers, but Lavrentin, a decorated veteran of Afghanistan and Iran, had been sent as a token of the importance of this operation. More men could not be spared from the fight against the Pan-Turanians, even to retrieve vital Blueprint technology; and besides, space had been limited by Roulade and his gaggle of technicians, and the extra fuel cells the Hercules had to carry to make the flight from Keflavik and return.

"Yes, Doctor," Thijs Van Thyssel said. "Surely we can provide for you all the security you need."

At the other end of the room, the other Liberators stood around drinking coffee and watching the brass confer. It was midnight, but they were still exalted by the evening's work.

"Hadn't had it in so long," Cowboy said, "my cock was so hard a bobcat couldn't scratch it."

Luttwak slapped him on a mountainous shoulder. "You're truly a prodigy, my friend. I did not believe you actually could fit that organ of yours into her rectum like that."

"Human body's a wonderful thing," Cowboy said. "Real flexible like."

Neil Corbin sat on a table edge to one side, eating one of his prepackaged organic ration packs from the vehicle, his fine nostrils pinched with distaste. Neither he nor Van Thyssel had taken part in the rape for different reasons.

"A pity we had to kill her," Peter Lynch murmured. "She really was a lovely creature in spite of that ludicrous get-up."

Pirelli sneered. "Of course we had to kill her. You do not understand terror."

"Thank God for small favors."

Cowboy waved his cup at the tall, blond, and classically handsome Soviet officer. "How long you think it'll take the Guardians to polish off his pretty boys?"

"You are giving our opposite numbers too much credit, I think," said Luttwak, missing the nuance of the tense Cowboy used. "They have hardly made an impressive showing so far."

But Peter had missed nothing. "How long *will* it take the Guardians? Surely you don't think they'll interfere at this stage of the game?"

"He's mad," Corbin said.

Pirelli uttered a brassy, yipping laugh. "The Guardians! Ha! They are finished, they are nothing, they are—how do you say in English? *Kaputt*. They will slink away and hide now until we hunt them down and make of them the end."

"Or maybe their countrymen will do the job in a fever of patriotism, and save us the trouble," Luttwak said. "You heard their little president earlier."

"Maybe so," said Cowboy, "maybe not."

"But is it not the plan?" Pirelli demanded.

"Yup."

"And hasn't the plan worked without flaw?"

"Why, surely, Luigi. You Marighela boys always have things your own way till it's time for the oppressors to step in, and then your little schemes all go to hell in a handbasket. Way I figure is, we done just about reached the repression phase, and the Guardians are just the boys to do the repressin'."

They stared at him, thunderstruck. "You mean you didn't believe everything would go as planned?" Luttwak asked.

"Course not. Don't be silly."

"The Chairman himself approved this plan," Luttwak said darkly.

"Why did you participate, if you didn't think it would work?" Peter demanded.

"I'm just a good ole boy. I do like I'm told. I just ride along with the rest of you fellas, 'cause it gives me a chance to fuck things and blow things up."

"Mad," Corbin said.

"I'm forced to agree," Peter said. "Bothering us is the furthest thing from the Guardians' minds right now."

"And if they do interfere . . ." Luttwak held his two fists up end to end and made a gesture like wringing a chicken's neck.

"You got that right, Bunky," Cowboy said. "Only

question is whose heads are gonna get popped off."

"Mother fuck," Billy McKay said.

Tom Rogers lay on his belly beside him, peering through binoculars at the factory below and to the east. The icy nighttime wind crawled down inside their parkas, but neither took any notice. They had plenty of anger to keep them warm.

Banks of bright lights had been erected everywhere around the hangars and attendant structures. Tiny figures, bundled against the cold, moved puposefully back and forth in their glare. Even on this hill eight hundred meters away, they could hear the thrum of a portable diesel generator.

"The bastards are bold. You gotta give them that." McKay shook his head. "But why Chairman Max is sendin' his boys halfway around the world to swipe a goddam prefab housing plant is way the hell beyond me."

"We overlooked something," Tom said.

"No shit. But they overlooked something worse."

"What's that, Billy?"

"They left us alive."

During the day, the Guardians kept watch in shifts, counting heads and getting every detail of deployment noted down. They noted twenty-three technician types, a dozen men and one officer in distinctive VDV combat fatigues, and six men dressed in winter-pattern camouflage coveralls of a markedly different design.

During the day, one or more of these six would enter a vehicle parked next to the brick administration building. The vehicle was a Cadillac Gage Super Commando, identical to Mobile One except that instead of a pair of stubby turret weapons, it had a single 20-mm cannon with a long slim barrel. Its presence cleared up a lot of mysteries.

McKay was on watch about 1330 when a patrol on

foot came across the hill he was hiding on. His ass was hanging very much out in the breeze. Mobile One was parked in a draw a kilometer away where it would probably be safe from detection. He was totally out of touch with the other Guardians; the mysterious bad guys obviously had their commo wrapped up as thoroughly as they used to have the FSE's. They didn't dare risk any traffic on their communicators that might have given their presence away. The enemy was clearly overconfident. They didn't want to spoil that.

He found a crack between two boulders and wedged his huge body into it, flattened like a lizard's. He thanked Christ it was him on watch instead of Casey or Sloan. Good as they were, they were not quite the best at this sort of snooping and pooping. He and Rogers were. He huddled his MP-5 against him and pretended he was a shrub.

The little Heckler & Koch submachine gun had a silencer built right in. It was a murder weapon, not a serious fighting tool. Any kind of firefight would burn the silencer out, and it couldn't take much of the knocking around that combat entails. But it was just peachy if you had to pop one or two bad guys who were getting too nosy for your health. On a scout like this, you didn't get into serious firefights, because if you did, you didn't get out of them.

Being a shrub he took very seriously, although he did not normally put much faith in mystic oingo-boingo. At the time the SEALs were infiltrating North Vietnam under OPLAN 34, they had discovered that pretending to be part of the scenery, envisioning yourself as part of the scenery, projecting the thought that you were part of the scenery, helped make the bad guys accept you as part of the scenery. Whether it was because of your psychic emanations or because concentrating real hard on being a shrub helped you stay absolutely still or what, in McKay's experience it worked.

They passed within thirty meters of him, four

troopies in blue berets carrying stubby little AKR assault rifles. They weren't what made him stare; he'd seen plenty of Soviet paratroops, even here in the United States, when the Effsees first arrived. But accompanying them was one of the most gigantic human beings he'd ever seen.

The guy looked like the Pillsbury Doughboy stuffed into combat cammies. He had on hornrims and a pack on his back and, yes, by God, a single-action cowboy pistol in a holster beneath his starboard love handle. McKay's first reaction was that the opposition had to be pretty hard up to resort to using a fat wad of blubber like that.

But the vast man moved over the treacherous rocky ground as noiselessly as smoke, with a sureness Tom Rogers might have envied, and he carried his long black FN-FAL ready in his hands, not slung. He was a professional.

He was more than that. He was a legend.

Fuckin' A, it's the Cowboy, McKay thought. And he didn't dare think it too loud. He concentrated on shrubbery until they went away.

"The Cowboy," Tom Rogers said. "Son of a bitch." And Tom Rogers *never* cussed.

In the shadowy world of dirty war, there are certain denizens who, despite swaddlings of secrecy, have legends spring up about them. Green Beret Thomas Rogers had been one. So had Billy McKay, both in Force RECON and in the mixed covert-ops group known as Studies and Observations Group, Southwest Asia Command. And so had the Cowboy.

Nobody knew his real name. He was former Rangers, former Green Berets, who served in SOG-SWAC about the same time as McKay. *Cowboy* was a dirty-war trade term of derision for the type of uncontrollable hairy-ass operative that line of work too often attracted. But *the* Cowboy took those undesirable characteristics and raised them to the level of art. From Tripoli to Tehran to Toulon, his name was spoken in mixed terms of disgust and admiration.

Eventually his excesses overreached even the necessarily lax standards of SOG-SWAC. He was cashiered not long after McKay collected the wound that took him out of the conventional military and into command of the Guardians. He had dropped out of sight.

Now he'd resurfaced. Even though McKay had never laid eyes on him before, he had no doubt in the world.

"He's that good?" Sloan asked, worried. The three of them were huddled in Mobile One. Casey was holding down the hilltop a klick away.

"He's better," Tom Rogers said.

It took Sloan a few seconds to get the next question out: "Can we take them, if they're all like him?"

"If there were six of them that good, then hell, no," McKay said.

Sloan's eyes got round at his leader's admission. He never thought he'd live to see the day when Billy McKay would say that less than a battalion of *anybody* could take the Guardians.

"But there aren't six like him on that team. There's barely six that good in the world. There's us, and him, and maybe one or two more. Our pal Vesensky was, before Case greased him."

"That's a relief," Sloan said ironically.

McKay shrugged. "Besides, what the hell have we got to lose? We're fucking outcasts, man. Better to die taking what vengeance we can than spend the rest of our lives being hunted like rabid dogs by our own people."

"Much as I hate to say it," Sloan said, "you're right."

McKay thought back over what he knew of the Cowboy's propensities, and he thought of what had been done to Cassie. "One thing," he said.

"What's that?"

"When it all comes down, the big fucker's mine."

"You're welcome to him, McKay," Sloan said with feeling.

"They're out there," Cowboy said. His high-pitched voice barely carried over the whine of battery-powered hand vacuums sucking remnants of radioactive dust off the machinery inside the hangar.

"Come off it," Corbin scoffed.

But Van Thyssel regarded him narrowly. He'd learned to trust Cowboy's intuitions. "Where?"

Cowboy shrugged. "I don't know exactly. But they're there. I could smell 'em."

Van Thyssel exchanged looks with the Australian. Corbin rolled his eyes.

And for once, Van Thyssel agreed with Corbin. Cowboy was mad, after all. You just had to take it into account.

"Come," he said, touching Cowboy's arm. "Let's go find something to eat and forget all this."

And Cowboy put back his head and whinnied a laugh.

CHAPTER
SEVENTEEN

Walking the perimeter with his rifle slung, Grigori Pavlovich stopped dead in his tracks. In the predawn darkness he had almost tripped over the form sprawled on frozen earth from which the snow had mostly melted.

"Ivan Aleksandrovich?" he asked tentatively. "Private Kurazov?" As if the winter-camouflaged parka and the Krinkov strapped across the broad back left any room for uncertainty.

Still, he knelt and rolled the motionless figure onto its back. Kurazov's slightly Asiatic eyes stared without sight at the stars overhead. The front of his parka was soaked in blood. His throat had been cut.

Grigori Pavlovich turned his head toward the brightly lit buildings three hundred meters away, opened his mouth to scream a warning, forgetting the walkie-talkie hung in its holster on his web gear. But what came out of his mouth was a fully jacketed 7.62-mm bullet followed by assorted bits of brain and bone. He collapsed in the dirt like a marionette whose strings have all been snipped at once.

• • •

Five hundred meters away, Casey Wilson held the still figure in his telescopic sight long enough to confirm it was down for good. Not that he needed to; he'd felt the shot was good the instant he squeezed it off. But he'd been trained not to take chances.

He shifted the rifle slightly to bring the pit dug at the outer edge of the illuminated area into his field of vision. The computer-enhanced scope showed him the bulky tube of an old-style starlight scope, pointed off somewhere to his left. Next to the operator an RPK-74 machine gun rested on butt and bipod.

Casey pressed the SEND button on his communicator twice: all clear. McKay and Rogers rose from the ground between the walking perimeter and the observation post and rushed forward. Leaving Sam Sloan, who was huddled among rocks and scrub barely fifty meters from where Casey had just dropped the sentry, to keep an eye on the OP with his own high-tech night-vision device, he went back to scanning the distant buildings. The microcomputer built into his scope automatically stepped down the gain, adjusting to increased illumination.

The Soviet security team had three men walking the perimeter and three more in dugouts equipped with the night scopes, machine guns, and field telephones, arranged in an equilateral triangle around the facility. It wasn't an optimum arrangement, but it did give them total coverage, if not much overlap. They had two more men walking a complicated but regular beat among the buildings, and the last four were presumably asleep. It was the best that could be done with their limited numbers.

A dit-dah-dit popped in the back of his skull. Sam had just seen the tripod-mounted starlight scope in the nearest pit swing back toward McKay and Rogers.

Casey turned his attention back toward the pit. Because he knew where to look he had little difficulty picking out the prone figures of his two companions. They lay pressed to the earth scarcely thirty meters from the pit, thinking shrub thoughts for all they were worth.

Since somebody called the pits on their phones from time to time, they planned to leave the observer unmolested as long as possible. Had a Russian been on the other end, it would have been an easy call, since Russians did everything by the book and would have phoned at precise intervals. Apparently one of the six mystery men handled the checks, however, since they came instead at random.

Now Casey had left it as long as possible. He touched a button on the side of the scope with one gloved finger. Glowing crosshairs appeared in the middle of the field. He centered them on the head behind the mounted night-vision device as it swung right, took a deep breath, let some of it out, and squeezed the trigger.

It broke crisply. The bullet came out of the sound and flash suppressor screwed onto the rifle's bull barrel. The wind ate the rippling crack the supersonic projectile made traveling over broken earth. It splashed home in the observer's skull. He convulsed and fell to the side, out of sight.

Click, click. McKay and Rogers rushed forward. They'd heard the sound the projectile made as it passed over their heads—a supersonic round can't be silenced completely, only the loud and unmistakable report of the actual shot. McKay went to his belly, covering with his M-60, as Rogers dropped into the pit with his leaf-shaped Gerber knife in hand. The double-edged Gerber was his sentry-killing tool; like McKay, Rogers carried a Kabar for actual fighting. Tom was an artist with a blade.

Tom emerged from the pit, tucking the knife away. He didn't have to wipe it clean; Casey had made another perfect shot. McKay worked his arm into the sling he'd rigged on his Maremont, while Tom slung his Galil

SAR. They both drew their .45s and screwed silencers onto the special extra-long tapped barrels they'd dropped into them before setting out. Then they got up and started forward again into the ocean of light.

They were halfway across the 150-meter skirt of illumination which surrounded the plant, just where it was starting to get bright, when the telephone in the pit behind them rang.

The two Guardians took off running as fast as they could for the buildings. The phone rang twice more and a klaxon began to bleat.

No sooner had Luttwak hit the alarm than Cowboy materialized in the doorway of the command center set up in the brick administration building. Though he was supposed to be asleep, he was fully dressed and armored, carrying an Uzi submachine gun.

A jack-o'-lantern grin split his face. "I told you assholes they'd be here," he said and vanished.

Cursing him, Luttwak leapt to his feet and grabbed his FN.

When he was on watch Corbin liked to have a place where he could dig in, set down his rifle's bipod, and prepare himself like a proper sniper. Unfortunately, this bloody factory was set up so that no one vantage point commanded the whole perimeter. He was reduced to wandering about with his rifle slung like a mere sentry.

At the sound of the alarm he moved instinctively west. The hills curved clear around to the north, but he had a gut feeling that trouble was coming from the west. In the SAS he'd learned to trust his gut; the last time he'd failed to do so he'd gotten tagged meeting his contact man in Lüneberg, and had to shoot down two West German counterintelligence men and do a quick fade east of the Elbe.

He didn't move all the way up. The other side might have snipers, too. Instead, he kept the administration building ahead and left and went to ground behind a four-meter square brick structure enclosing electrical transformers. Unknowingly, he placed himself just out of Casey Wilson's field of vision and fire.

At the amplified honking of the klaxon, Peter Lynch, Pirelli, and Van Thyssel rolled out of their bunks in the building which held the commissary.

"Where's Cowboy?" Van Thyssel asked.

Pulling on his Kevlar vest, Peter shrugged. "I don't know. But I gather he was right all along, wasn't he?"

But his commander and Pirelli were already out the door, headed for their vehicle.

McKay and Rogers hugged the side of the administration building, staying below the level of the windows. Both men were breathing heavily. It was hard to stay in shape riding all day in an armored car. Besides, each was wearing a full Hard Corps IV vest, Kevlar with ceramic-steel inserts, which supposedly would stop even a 7.62 round, as well as being weighed down with weapons. It was a hefty load to carry.

McKay jerked his head left. Bent over, they moved down around the south end of the building. As they did so, they heard the familiar roar of a V-450 engine firing up to north and east of them.

Sam Sloan sat with his knees drawn up and his elbows propped inside them, to provide the most stable possible firing platform for his grenade launcher. He felt mighty sacrificial out here by himself.

Plan A was for him to help Casey cover while the other two made it to the buildings, then for Casey and them to cover while he went in. This was Plan B. He'd stick where he was and then move up to join his buddies or pull back to help Casey with the car as circumstances dictated. He was guiltily hoping for the latter. He was in no hurry to go racing across a broad well-lit parking lot toward a whole bunch of alerted enemies.

He heard a diesel going, and then a V-450 came skidding out from among the buildings. It stopped, and its long gun spat projectiles at the hills with a ripping snarl. Sam aimed and fired the HEDP round he had up the spout.

High-explosive rounds from the machine cannon cracked off among the rocks above and behind him like lightning. The enemy driver was a pro; no sooner had his gunner triggered his burst than he gunned the engine and darted ahead. Sam's grenade cratered pavement where the car had been an instant earlier.

It was damn near a four-hundred-meter shot, crowding the limit of his M-203's range, and anyway the target moved, but Sam cursed himself for missing. He was a naval gunnery officer, after all, not some damn landlubber amateur. The short-barreled grenade launcher wasn't a twelve-inch gun with computer-aided radar aiming, but just as a real artist should be able to draw with his fingertip on a wet tablecloth, Sam's pride demanded he excel with the implement at hand. He broke open the launcher and reached in the many-pocketed vest for another round.

Whistling tunelessly to himself, Corbin pointed his rifle toward where the outsized muzzle flash had briefly appeared. That was another wretched thing about this job—he couldn't use a starlight scope among all these lights without burning the damned thing out. He had to rely on a plain telescopic sight with an extra-wide objective lens and his own superlative vision.

They were enough. He found his target, sitting in firing position behind a bush. The head was partially blocked by a weapon, so he aimed for the center of the chest and clicked the set trigger. His forefinger brushed the firing trigger. The big Walther pulled back against his shoulder.

The weighted barrel rose only slightly, falling back on

line in time for him to see his target rolling over. *Bull's eye*.

Tom Rogers halted at the rear of the administration building, holding up a warning hand. Cautiously, McKay joined him, taking a three-second look around the corner. Twenty meters away a figure in camouflaged coveralls lay prone on the ground behind a chunky black bull-pup rifle with an outsized scope.

McKay traded glances with Rogers. The silencers screwed onto their pistols blocked the sights, and twenty meters was too damned far to try point-shooting a handgun. McKay laid down his pistol. Everybody knew they were there anyway, there was no convenient way to carry a silenced pistol except in your hand, and there was no damned time to unscrew the beast.

He unslung the Maremont. He held it by fore and aft pistol grips, snugged it under his right elbow, and stepped out around the corner.

"Bandits approaching from due west," Corbin sub-vocalized in response to his commander's request for a sit-rep. "I just bagged one."

Somewhere out of his sight the V-450 halted momentarily to cut loose with another blast into the hills. "Have you spotted any others?"

He was about to answer in the negative when he caught motion from the corner of his eye. He didn't even try to swing the bulky rifle around, just rolled away, clawing for his sidearm.

McKay's burst caught him squarely in the torso. The 7.62 slugs drove stalagmites of elastic Kevlar deep into his body before bursting the tips like pimples. The first Liberator casualty died with holes in him you could put your hand in.

Technology triumphs again, Sloan thought muzzily as he picked himself up. As advertised, the curved ceramic-steel plates of his vest had stopped the slug that caught him under the right arm, and it didn't feel as if more than two or three of his ribs were busted.

Of course, if the bullet had struck a couple of centimeters further left, it would have been a different story. It would have hit one of his 40-mm grenades. Thinking about it made him wince worse than the pain that stabbed through him every time he took a breath.

"Scratch one sniper," Billy McKay's voice said in his ear. "Casey, Sam, get Mobile One and take out that car. We'll worry about the rest."

Gratefully, Sam turned and started scrambling back up the slope. As if to warn him not to get complacent, 20-mm shells lashed the hillside a hundred meters to his right. He zigged left and ran faster.

McKay raced across bare ground from the administration building toward one of the hangars. A Soviet paratrooper popped out from behind the metal structure, firing his AKR from the hip, barely ten meters from him. McKay got the range first. He fired the Maremont like an outsized submachine gun. The trooper spun around and went down.

Gunfire cracked from deeper inside the compound. McKay threw himself down behind the man he'd shot. As he did, glass blew out of a darkened window behind him and a bullet cracked past his ear. He rolled frantically left.

Tom Rogers took a step forward from the corner of the building and sprayed the windows with automatic fire.

"Shit," McKay said. The boy up front was still firing him up, with little dust geysers popping out all around him. Caught between two fires wasn't a good place to be. Trusting Tom to clear his backfield, he rolled over onto his stomach and blazed away at the muzzle flashes ahead of him.

• • •

Lying on his stomach on a thin carpet with chunks of glass lying all over him like heavy jagged snow, Luttwak congratulated himself on being alive. Had he acted the way the fools did in the movies, smashing out the glass and bellying right up the window to stick his rifle out and fire, he'd be dead this instant. But the heavy bullets from his Belgian-made FN broke glass just fine, and when you fired them from a couple of meters inside the room the enemy had a much harder time seeking you out with his fire.

He picked himself up, placing his hands carefully to avoid cutting them on broken glass. He could hear the machine gun bellowing not twenty meters away, and its muzzle flash cast spastic shadows on the wall. He moved to another window.

Something thumped on the cheap carpet behind him. *Grenade,* he thought, without terrific urgency. His Kevlar body armor would stop fragments, and grenades were seldom lethal anyway. But his legs were unprotected, so he threw himself to the floor.

Whoever was outside had held the grenade after pulling the pin. It went off before he hit the floor.

Sam Sloan wasn't a former marathon runner for nothing. Encumbered as he was, in the dark and uphill, he still made the five hundred meters back to Casey's position in less than a minute and a half. He had incentive.

Casey nodded briskly to him as he came panting over the top. Down on the flat the enemy V-450 was still darting in and out and spraying fire into the hills. They pulled back to Mobile One, now parked twenty meters back from the crest.

Inside, a heavily sedated Bender lay strapped down like loose gear. They'd been afraid to drop him off with either settlers or natives for fear they'd kill him out of hand as an accomplice of the hated Guardians. It made Tom nuts, but it had to be.

• • •

The room was burning. Luttwak was burning. Choking on stinging, dense smoke, he tore his blazing coveralls from his body.

A thousand tiny white stars shone through the smoke around him. Everything in the room had been impregnated with flakes of phosphorus, burning at a temperature that could melt steel.

He hacked away shreds of the uniform with his knife. Only the upper half was afire, thank God; a desk had protected the lower part of his body. He was safe.

Then he felt a multifold burning like a hundred fire ants crawling all over his body. He looked down. His armor vest was a constellation of malignant stars. The phosphorus ate through, welding the plastic-fiber armor to his flesh with searing agony.

He shrieked, clawing at the vest. Some of the flakes had burned through to his body, burning their way inside him, the China Syndrome on a microminiature scale and multiplied by twenty, by fifty.

Then, to his great good fortune, Tom Rogers appeared at the window and shot him through the head.

CHAPTER
EIGHTEEN ——————————

Tom dashed forward to the corner of the hangar. McKay was now dueling with at least two opponents, neither of whom seemed intimidated by the firepower of his powerful machine gun.

Tom tossed another white phosphorus grenade. He wasn't planning on catching anybody with the fragments, though that would be nice. He was using it for what it was nominally intended for, as a smoke grenade.

It produced a brilliant white flash and a starfish of white smoke. The arms of the starfish turned into tentacles waving in the air; the buildings kept the wind from tearing them apart too quickly. He ran forward, dodging through the smoke while McKay fired high, busting caps to give the opposition something to think about.

There were two Soviet paras firing around the corner of the cinder-block building. Standing on the far side of the building, Tom prepped another grenade, smaller than the Willie Peter grenades. He stuck his arm around the corner and bounced the grenade toward the two.

It went off a few meters in front of their faces with a

whole bunch of sound and fury and blinding light. It
didn't hurt them; it was a stun bomb. It had the desired
effect of blinding and confusing them. Then Tom
stepped forward and killed them with two quick shots
each.

He called McKay forward on the communicator. The
burly ex-Marine had just about reached him when the
strange V-450 came prowling in among the buildings,
hungry for Guardian meat. The bad guys spotted them
at once. The 20 mike-mike came around. Tom and
McKay hurled themselves across an infinite five meters
to a door in the flank of the hangarlike structure as a
burst shattered concrete blocks behind them.

They may have been dodging for their lives, but they
were still Guardians. There was no time for stun grenades; they jerked the door open and went in, McKay
high and left and firing from the hip, Tom low and
right.

That was a good thing. Because the Cowboy was
waiting for them.

A burst cut the doorway at belt-buckle height, a millisecond too late to nail McKay. But the Cowboy's reflexes were like a rattlesnake's. Two rounds of his
second burst caught McKay over the lats as he quit
shooting and dived for the deck.

A burst from Tom's Galil blew apart the camera eyes
of a wheeled robot with two viselike claws. But Cowboy's vast bulk had already melted into the thicket of
machinery.

McKay lay behind a couple of crates and his Maremont. He was glad for the heavily armored vest, though
it was a royal pain in the ass to wear. At that range those
nasty little 9-mm bullets would have driven enough
kinetic energy through simple Kevlar to hurt a hell of a
lot. As it was, he just felt as if he'd been punched real
hard.

"Helluva way to make a living," he muttered. He got
up and started moving forward.

•   •   •

"Damn, damn, damn!" Sloan exclaimed. "Where did they *go?*"

Casey had pulled Mobile One right up to the crest of the hill so Sam could cover the factory with the turret armament. Now he was doing so, only to find no targets.

"He must be in among the buildings."

"Yeah. McKay, Tom, where are you?" He couldn't very well start blasting holes in the factory at random without knowing where his buddies were.

The fact that this seemed, impossibly, to be a genuine twenty-four-carat Blueprint facility never entered his head. They were outlaws. They hadn't come to preserve or rescue techno-goodies, no matter how essential. They had come to kill people.

Unfortunately, the people they were trying to kill also had it in mind to kill them. And they were good at it, too.

The observation post on the far side of the factory was obscured by buildings. The one to the north and east, however, was in visual range, and its occupant had been scanning the whole line of hills since the alarm sounded.

He was a professional. He knew what to look for, and his eyes were keen. Even though the V-450 was placed in the hull-down position, with little more than its turret outlined against the night sky, he spotted it.

Nobody answered the phone. He was ready for that. He pulled the mike off the walkie-talkie holstered at his side and got an immediate response. Without haste, he recited a set of coordinates.

The enemy V-450 rolled out from behind a building, and it came out shooting. Casey jerked the car into reverse as a burst of shells hit the front glacis, its steep slope accentuated by the angle at which the vehicle rested. They exploded in an upward cascade of fire, unable to penetrate.

Sam yelped in alarm as one skipped off the front armor and blew a hole in the turret, shredding his right sleeve with white-hot fragments. Then the hill was between them and harm.

"These guys are pretty good," Casey admitted.

"But not *that* good," Sloan said. He was unhurt, and the adrenal rush of having his invincible iron shell violated was catalyzing from fear to anger. "We've been spotted. Shift us a few meters north."

"Aye-aye, man."

McKay and Tom advanced in short rushes along steel avenues, playing cat-and-mouse with their enormous enemy. Three times one or both traded brief fire with the renegade, but neither side scored any hits, though they blew an extravagant number of holes in who knew how many thousand bucks worth of your latest state-of-the-art prefab housing manufacturing robots. It was a stalemate; the antagonists were just too good. But by virtue of the fact that there were two of them, the Guardians kept Cowboy from slipping around a flank or between them. Gradually, inexorably, they drove him to the eastern end of the structure.

They reached the five-meter clear space by the wall. Tom flipped out a stun bomb. McKay let it flash off, then stepped around with his machine gun ready. Motion fluttered at the brink of his peripheral vision.

He wheeled and fired. Scarlet splashes appeared on the white coveralls of a pair of technicians, and they screamed through their respirator masks and died.

The man-sized door stood open. Cowboy had flown the coop.

With an agility belying its dinosaur mass, Mobile One popped back up on the ridge. Sam Sloan triggered a measured burst. Casey rolled her back to safety as the enemy car flailed the hilltop in impotent fury.

The observer in the OP to the north and east died in a torrent of exploding steel and white phosphorus. The defenders weren't the only people who had the terrain mapped out. Sloan had put in his time among the rocks during the day, and knew with mathematical precision where the observation pit lay. The rest was child's play.

Casey opened the side hatch, slipped out, and moved cautiously up to the top of the hill.

Tom pitched a Willie Peter into the space between the hangars, in case Cowboy or anybody else had cute ideas about surprising them. When it went off they dashed across an interval that appeared to have been dusted by a fall of burning snow.

The door stood open. McKay threw in a stun grenade. It was Tom's turn to go high and left, McKay low and right.

Gunfire clawed at them. Some clever boy had shut his eyes when the stun bomb hit the concrete floor. He was blasting at Tom from behind a manipulator robot with one of those nasty little AKR Krinkovs.

McKay was hugging the pavement behind one of the robot forklifts. It seemed pretty solid. The housing of the manipulator robot, on the other hand, appeared to be thin-gauge metal. *Let's see how much of the inside of that hooter is solid and how much is air*, he thought, then hosed it down.

There was a clatter of metal on cement. McKay peered along the floor. He saw an outstretched hand and part of a body in Soviet camouflage lying on the far side of the manipulator robot. He dropped the muzzle and fired quick, cautious bursts, splashing the rounds in a shallow angle off the pavement until a jerk of the body told him he'd hit. He wasn't taking any chances.

Tom covered him as he moved forward. A man wearing a Soviet captain's insignia lay on his back. He must have been a handsome sonofabitch before some inconsiderate bastard blew off half his head.

Carefully, Pirelli eased the V-450 forward, hugging the side of the administration building. He flicked between low-light TV and active and passive IR. The enemy wasn't showing himself.

In the turret, Thijs van Thyssel waited with a gloved thumb on the firing switch. He felt calm, supremely confident. At moments like this he could forget about the sordid task he'd volunteered for and the beautiful compact flower garden he'd left behind in Holland alike. This was what he lived for: honest, clean combat. The highest form of art: a contest of consummate professionals. Not a war of rape and torture and assassination.

He knew that the dirty parts were necessary to the unification of Europe and the world, the eventual abolition of war—war like the thermonuclear bombardment that had robbed him of his wife and two daughters. That had robbed so many of their lives and loved ones.

"Where do you think they'll turn up?" Pirelli asked. Nervousness trilled in his voice. He wasn't like Van Thyssel; he didn't enjoy the boiling rush of combat. The other parts were the ones he liked.

"It doesn't matter," Van Thyssel said. "We'll find them."

The Mark-19 automatic grenade launcher in the Guardians' V-450 was powerful, but it had a long, looping trajectory and low muzzle velocity. Opposed to that was the 20-mm gun with its high rate of fire, flat trajectory, and shorter flight time. In a battle where milliseconds counted, he felt sure he could score the vital first hits that meant the difference between killing or being killed.

"They'd better come soon," Pirelli whined.

"Don't worry. They will."

"I've got them," Casey said. "South side of that

brick administration building.''

The servomotors made little peevish noises as Sloan elevated the Mark-19 and traversed the turret. His mathematician's brain calculated the angle at which the car was parked, the angle of elevation of the launcher, the flight path of the 40-mm rounds. Then he threw in a few seconds of Kentucky windage; he was indulging in an elaborate form of guesswork and knew it.

It was highly educated guesswork, though. He grinned and punched the butterfly trigger.

Forty-mm rounds fell on the V-450 like hail. Pirelli just had time to scream in surprise, and then an HEDP round struck almost perpendicular to the front glacis. Its shaped-charge warhead drove a lance of incandescent copper through the armor plate and vaporized his flesh from his sternum to his thighs.

They had reached the far side of the last hangar. Hunkered next to a robot forklift, McKay hurled a stun grenade. Tom moved forward into the open, ducking left out of the aisle where McKay crouched.

Everything happened at once. Fire slashed at Tom from an office to his left. A round caught him in the ribs but hit an insert and failed to penetrate. He let the momentum turn him around, fired and saw a man in cammie coveralls drop a small submachine gun and duck back, cursing and clutching a bleeding arm.

McKay was lunging up to support him when a stun bomb went off in their faces. The next thing McKay knew, a heavy weight dropped on him from above and carried him crashing to the cement.

Thijs van Thyssel was surrounded by fire and choking smoke. Ammunition for the 20-mm gun was cooking off in a storage bin, searing the right side of his body and peppering him with splinters.

He fought the top hatch open, hurled himself upward

to the clear cold air; he was savagely burned, half blinded, but alive.

A freshet of .50-caliber machine gunfire swept down from the distant ridge and tore the life out of him. His right arm landed fifteen meters from the car.

McKay dug hard with an elbow and heard a grunt. He reached back blind, found a short-haired head, seized an ear and twisted. Somebody cried out in anger and pain and he felt a knife grate against his armor plating. He got his other hand on the head and rolled onto his back, dragging its owner around on top of him. Huge splotches of purple afterimage still obscured his vision. But he didn't need to see to break his opponent's neck with one ferocious jerk.

Over the ringing in his ears, he heard footsteps. Slow and heavy. Very heavy. Moving as little as he could, he reached to his belt for his last grenade.

The footsteps stopped. He pulled the pin, hoping the body atop him muffled the sound of the spring-driven lever that set off the fuse. He began to count. If he guessed wrong, he was in a world of hurt.

"That's you, McKay, ain't it?" It was a high, oddly fluting voice with a West Texas accent you could scrape off your shoe. "Well, it's time you come on out and faced the music. Your little buddy's lying out on the floor with a bullet in his head, and you can't hide under no Russki stiff for long."

McKay rolled the grenade toward the voice and made himself very, very small beneath the dead paratrooper.

The Cowboy uttered a piping shriek. He turned and fled. The white phosphorus grenade went off behind him.

The screaming had subsided. McKay hauled himself out from under the Soviet corpse, staggered forward, choking on swirling smoke, trying not to inhale any. Phosphorus could get inside you and turn your bones the consistency of rubber. The smoke wasn't supposed to do that, but he was damned if he was taking any chances with that shit.

He was still blinking away balls of afterimage when he found Tom Rogers lying behind tumbled barrels of industrial-strength cleaner. The former Green Beret was sitting up, shaking his head. Blood gushed from a furrow that ran along his right temple as straight as if cut by a razor. His reflexes had been just a millisecond better than Cowboy's. It had saved his life.

He picked up his rifle. McKay collected his M-60 and went to the door. He peered out. In darkness just diluted by false dawn gray, he saw a man-shaped shadow lying thirty meters away, smouldering and glowing from a hundred phosphorus eyes.

Then movement caught his attention near the rocks a hundred meters away, perched on the cliff above the poorly named Little Dry Creek. A giant pallid form was just limping in among them.

McKay snap-fired a burst from his Maremont. It didn't even come close. "Shit," he said and raced forward.

Cowboy was smarter than Luttwak, or at least quicker to make the right moves. He'd also been farther from McKay's grenade, so that the phosphorus flakes hadn't punched clean through the tough fabric of the coveralls and into his Kevlar. He had skinned out of his uniform on the run, even though it meant leaving his web belt with knife and .44 Magnum behind.

It didn't matter. His glasses were gone, but that didn't matter either. He crouched down among the rocks and grinned. He didn't need perfect vision, and he didn't need weapons. He was the Cowboy.

"Come on out, cocksucker," McKay said. "Come out and die."

The rocks didn't answer him. He wasn't surprised.

He heard no sound but the wind and the rushing of the water thirty or forty meters below, and that didn't surprise him either. Cowboy would need far less background sound than that, either to sneak up on him or climb down the bluffs and escape.

McKay grinned. Neither did he. With his machine gun ready, he climbed up into the rocks.

They were tumbled boulders, inclining to slab shapes rather than round. McKay knew how to put his feet to avoid loose rock that might crunch or slip beneath his boots. He knew how to hug the masses thrusting up around him to make it hard to pick out his shape. And his eardrums had been ground down fine by years in the field, able to pick out the faintest alien sound.

It was his sense of smell that saved him.

He smelled burned hair. He spun as if a gyroscope had kicked in and brought the M-60 up to fire a burst into the figure looming over him like a fleshy white mountain.

The gun fired once, its flash illuminating a round face twisted with goblin glee, the bullet skimming a roll of flab and heading off for Alpha Centauri. Then it stopped. When the Soviet had jumped him the belt had gotten twisted inside the Aussie half-moon ammo box, and the next round hung up.

Cowboy brought a chunk of sandstone down and smashed the Maremont from McKay's hands. McKay jumped back, turned, and scrambled desperately away. The rock shattered against a boulder where his head had been a moment before.

He pulled himself up about eight centimeters from running right out onto air. The bluffs fell sheer to the surging white water. He turned around and lunged to the side to avoid an irresistible rush.

Cowboy's charge almost carried him over the edge. But he just stopped himself as if inertia didn't make him no never mind, turned about, and came for McKay as he crouched against the rock.

Can't let the fucker grapple me, McKay thought desperately. Huge as McKay was, the renegade dwarfed him. He put everything he had into a thrust kick straight into Cowboy's balls.

It stopped him. For about half the time it takes an eye to blink. Then he caught McKay's heel and yanked him off balance, right against his gigantic chest.

His arms went around McKay. He felt muscles like masses of rock moving within cushions of flab, enfolding him, tightening around him with drill-press pressure.

He tried to break away. His trapezius muscles swelled up into great buttresses between shoulder and jaw, and the veins stood out on his neck. He might as well have been trying to deadlift Mobile One. He butted his forehead furiously into Cowboy's face. Derisive laughter whistled through a broken nose, and then that desert-wide forehead was pressing down against McKay's, driving his head back until his neck muscles creaked while Cowboy leered at him with ghastly bloody lips.

Now it was a serious question as to which was going to give way first, McKay's spine or neck. For all his strength he couldn't loosen Cowboy's death grip by a fraction, or stop the relentless pressure forcing his head back until his cervical vertebrae made popping noises like corn on a hot stove.

"I'm gonna break you," Cowboy said, "then I'm gonna drop you."

"When . . . hell . . . shuts down . . . for Christmas," McKay grunted. He forced his right hand between his rock-hard belly and the enormous softness of Cowboy's, reaching crosswise for the handle of his Kabar. Cowboy sensed his intent, and his shoulders heaved like Atlas putting the earth like a shot, and McKay felt the bones of his back beginning to part. The knife came free and he turned his hand and drove it to the hilt into that huge gut.

Cowboy squealed and staggered back. McKay felt as if Mobile One had driven over him, but he had his rage and hatred to keep him going.

"This is for Vista," he bellowed, driving a front kick into Cowboy's belly.

"This is for the Freehold," he said, kicking him in the crotch so hard it lifted his feet from the stone.

"This is for Cassie," he yelled, and the ball of his boot caught the hilt of his knife and drove it almost out of sight.

"*And this is for fucking me!*" He put every gram of body weight and hatred into a spinning back kick that launched Cowboy clean off the edge of the bluff.

McKay went down, barely stopping himself from going over the edge. He watched the gigantic white body turn end over end, to vanish with a gargantuan splash in the greedy waters below.

With all the strength he had to his name, he got up and staggered back to where the defenders of the plant were emerging into milky dawnlight with their hands above their heads, under the watchful guns of the real Mobile One.

EPILOGUE

"I'm embarrassed not to have thought of it before," Dr. Jacob Morgenstern admitted over the long-distance line. "Imagine: it was the factory itself that was valuable, not what it produced. The most sophisticated and versatile manufacturing robots yet devised. This technology has the potential to rebuild the country almost overnight."

"I'm impressed," Billy McKay said sourly. His nose was broken, and he looked like a goddam raccoon with two huge black eyes, and only threats of physical violence had stopped Tom Rogers from cinching him into a neck brace.

They were parked in the lee of one of the hangarlike buildings, just holding down the pavement and waiting for a new team of specialists from Washington to come in. And to take charge of a dozen prisoners, including one of the FSE's top experts on the Blueprint for Renewal, three Soviet paratroopers, and one member of the counter-Guardian team that called itself the Liberators.

"They fooled all of us, Doctor," Sam said. "The

197

purloined-letter method of concealment—beautiful.''

"Jesus," McKay said.

"Yes, indeed," Morgenstern said, presumably not in response to McKay. There was a pause. "I'm afraid you've caused the President no little embarrassment.''

"Excuse us all to tears, Doctor," McKay said.

To their surprise, Morgenstern laughed. "I may be trusting too much to the security of our communications, given the events of the last few weeks, but I have to say it serves him right for rushing to make that foolish announcement.'' His tone darkened. "Or allowing himself to be rushed.''

Things had been touch and go for the Guardians, even after the fight at the factory was won. Even with a wounded and quite talkative Peter Lynch as a prisoner, even with the computer memory full of the Guardians' access codes captured intact from the damaged armored car, it had been no easy task to convince Washington what had really happened. It had taken the personal and acerbic intervention of Dr. Jacob Morgenstern with President MacGregor to even get him to review the exculpatory evidence the Guardians had found. Tide Camp was up in arms about the murder of Steve Tyler, and Maggie Connoly . . . well, Maggie Connoly seemed very disappointed to see them clear themselves.

The Guardians could almost sense Morgenstern shaking himself. "Well, enough of that. I had faith that you men were incapable of the treachery you were accused of, and that faith was justified.''

"Thank you, sir," Billy McKay said humbly and sincerely. There was nothing more to say.

"Washington informs me that the new recovery team will arrive tomorrow. Once you hand off to them, you're to return to the capital, bringing your prisoner for comprehensive interrogation.''

"Great," McKay said.

"And one more thing," the doctor said. "I'll do what I can to convince the Freeholders of your innocence.

They are allies too valuable to let slip through our fingers. Isn't that right, Lieutenant Wilson?"

Slumped in the driver's seat, Casey glanced up. "Huh?" Suddenly he grinned. "Yes, *sir,* sir. That's absolutely right."

"Morgenstern, out."

McKay shuffled his aches and pains around some and sighed. "Just one last bit of business to attend to."

The trial in New Billings was an anticlimax. It was held in the domed City Center, hastily repaired after the shelling by the Liberators. The defendants all stipulated to the facts of the case—they had raided the Absaroka camp, and caused deaths and injuries and property damage as follows, and so on. As president of the court, McKay refused to hear any arguments about the justification of either side's claims. When the man appointed to represent the settlers wanted to press the issue, the president of the court offered to smash his face in. The settlers' attorney—a real one, just as the natives' advocate was—declined to press the issue.

The tragic events of the last few days had knocked the vengefulness out of everybody for the moment—at least against anybody who wasn't one of the Liberators. Besides, as far as casualties went, raiders and defenders had come out about even. Nobody argued when the defendants were found guilty and sentenced to a year in custody, plus a healthy reparation payable in livestock.

McKay then pounded on the podium with a gavel—that was the one part he liked about this judicial shit, and he was gratified he'd had so many opportunities to do it, brief as the proceedings were—and announced that he was suspending the jail sentence of Michael Rutherford on condition that he opened good-faith negotiations with the settlers in his capacity as new head of the Montana People's Protective Association. His comrades were released into his custody.

"This court hereby recommends that any further outbreaks of unprovoked violence between the two communities be punished by death," McKay said. He hammered the gavel some more. "Court dismissed. Or adjourned. Or whatever the hell."

They drove past Bender's on the way back to the plant. Helpful customers had boarded up the shattered windows, but the famous sign looked pathetic, still hanging there on the side of the building. Its owner would survive, under care of a doctor in New Billings, but the Guardians had the feeling the loss of that sign pained him worse than his physical injuries.

Cassie's death troubled the tavern keeper so much that both Tom Rogers and the New Billings physician were afraid he'd fret himself into a decline. But there was nothing the Guardians could do about that.

For his part, Billy McKay tried not to think about Cassandra Morgan at all. That was best, he'd learned. He'd had more experience to learn from than he cared to think about.

"Is it going to work, man?"

"Huh?" McKay said, lifting his chin from his hand. "Is what gonna work?" he asked gruffly, though he was secretly grateful to Casey for distracting him from brooding.

"Back in New Billings. Do you think they'll work things out all right?"

"Yes," said Sam Sloan.

"No," said Billy McKay.

"But they accepted our order to negotiate."

"Yeah. Big fuckin' deal."

"But Redfeather's in charge in New Billings now," Casey pointed out.

"That's true. And I gotta admit he had his head fitted on straighter than just about anybody we've run into around here. But what's gonna happen when the hard-asses on one side or the other decide they've got a gutful of sweet reason and decide to go night-riding again?"

Sloan mulled it over, licked his lips, and shook his head. "I guess you don't believe in happy endings, McKay."

"Sure I do. We won, didn't we?" He shook his battered head. "It's happily ever after I don't buy."

Richard Austin
The Guardians £3.50

The first adventure in the blistering new series

World War III is over . . . and the ultimate battle for control
has begun.

From the blasted ruins of World War III came the Guardians . . .

Armed with awesome combat skills; equipped with the most
devastating weaponry ever devised; trained to hair-trigger tautness;
the Guardians have been entrusted with freedom's last hope . . .
. . . the top secret blueprint for renewal!

Their first task: to get the new President away from a ravaged
Washington to the mid-western fortress known as Heartland.

But between Washington and the impregnable fortress lie a
thousand miles of chaos . . .

Trial by Fire £3.50

The second adventure in the blistering new series

The Guardians' first task has been accomplished – the President is
safe in the fortress known as Heartland. Their next step: to hunt
down the hi-tech experts – for only they can put the Blueprint into
operation!

With time running out, is this Mission Impossible for the fighting
elite?

The future lies in their hands!

All Pan books are available at your local bookshop or newsagent, or can be ordered direct from the publisher. Indicate the number of copies required and fill in the form below.

Send to: **CS Department, Pan Books Ltd., P.O. Box 40, Basingstoke, Hants. RG21 2YT.**

or phone: 0256 469551 (Ansaphone), quoting title, author and Credit Card number.

Please enclose a remittance* to the value of the cover price plus: 60p for the first book plus 30p per copy for each additional book ordered to a maximum charge of £2.40 to cover postage and packing.

*Payment may be made in sterling by UK personal cheque, postal order, sterling draft or international money order, made payable to Pan Books Ltd.

Alternatively by Barclaycard/Access:

Card No.

Signature:

Applicable only in the UK and Republic of Ireland.

While every effort is made to keep prices low, it is sometimes necessary to increase prices at short notice. Pan Books reserve the right to show on covers and charge new retail prices which may differ from those advertised in the text or elsewhere.

NAME AND ADDRESS IN BLOCK LETTERS PLEASE:

....

Name ————————————————————————

Address ————————————————————————

————————————————————————————

————————————————————————————

————————————————————————————

3/87